# DANGEROUS PLANET

## Natural Disasters That Changed History

Written and Illustrated by
BRYN BARNARD

Crown Publishers ♛ New York

**Just the Big Ones**

*Some significant natural disasters*

- ● Natural disasters
- ● *Dangerous Planet* disasters
- ● Deadliest disasters

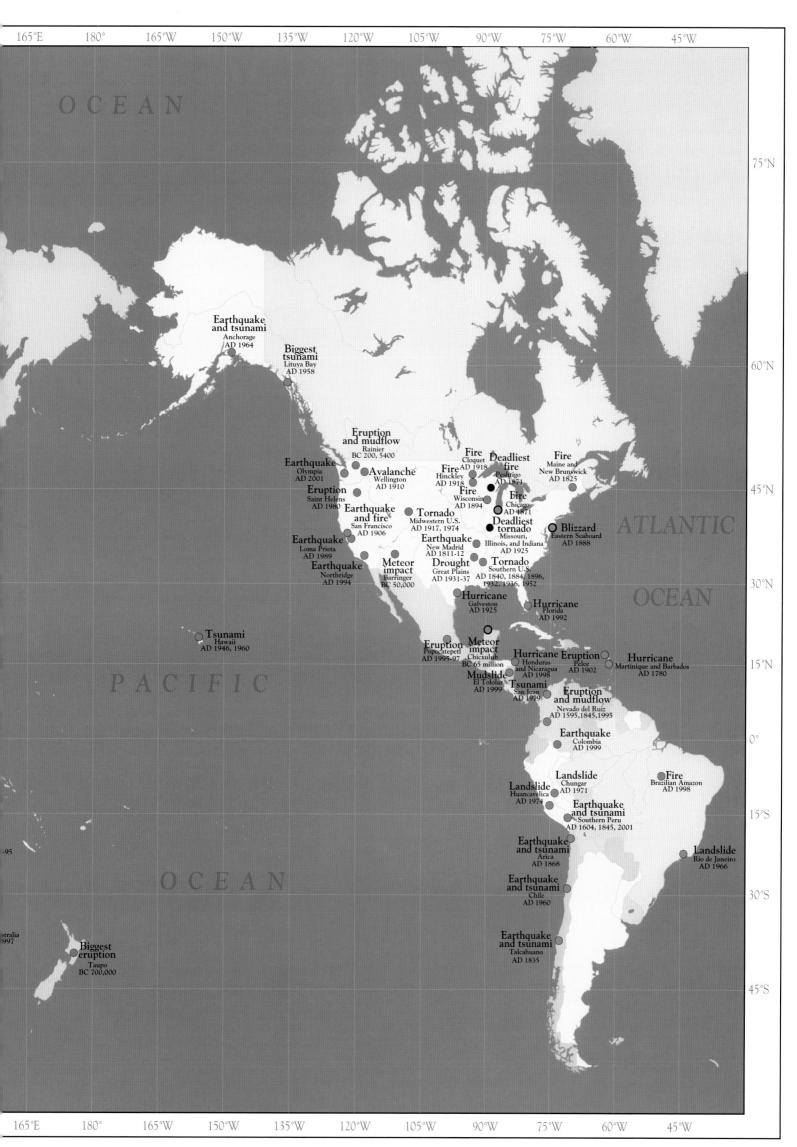

165°E   180°   165°W   150°W   135°W   120°W   105°W   90°W   75°W   60°W   45°W

75°N

60°N

**Earthquake and tsunami**
Anchorage
AD 1964

**Biggest tsunami**
Lituya Bay
AD 1958

**Eruption and mudflow**
Rainier
BC 200, 5400

**Earthquake**
Olympia
AD 2001

**Avalanche**
Wellington
AD 1910

**Fire**
Cloquet
AD 1918

**Deadliest fire**
Peshtigo
AD 1871

**Fire**
Maine and
New Brunswick
AD 1825

**Fire**
Hinckley
AD 1918

**Eruption**
Saint Helens
AD 1980

**Earthquake and fire**
San Francisco
AD 1906

**Fire**
Wisconsin
AD 1894

**Fire**
Chicago
AD 1871

**Tornado**
Midwestern U.S.
AD 1917, 1974

**Earthquake**
Loma Prieta
AD 1989

**Earthquake**
New Madrid
AD 1811-12

**Deadliest tornado**
Missouri,
Illinois, and Indiana
AD 1925

**Blizzard**
Eastern Seaboard
AD 1888

**Earthquake**
Northridge
AD 1994

**Meteor impact**
Barringer
BC 50,000

**Drought**
Great Plains
AD 1931-37

**Tornado**
Southern U.S.
AD 1840, 1884, 1896,
1932, 1936, 1952

ATLANTIC

**Hurricane**
Galveston
AD 1925

**Hurricane**
Florida
AD 1992

OCEAN

**Tsunami**
Hawaii
AD 1946, 1960

**Eruption**
Popocatepetl
AD 1995-97

**Meteor impact**
Chicxulub
BC 65 million

**Hurricane**
Honduras
and Nicaragua
AD 1998

**Eruption**
Pelee
AD 1902

**Hurricane**
Martinique and Barbados
AD 1780

PACIFIC

**Mudslide**
El Tololar
AD 1999

**Tsunami**
San Juan
AD 1979

**Eruption and mudflow**
Nevado del Ruiz
AD 1595,1845,1995

**Earthquake**
Colombia
AD 1999

**Fire**
Brazilian Amazon
AD 1998

**Landslide**
Chungar
AD 1971

**Landslide**
Huancavelica
AD 1974

**Earthquake and tsunami**
Southern Peru
AD 1604, 1845, 2001

**Landslide**
Rio de Janeiro
AD 1966

**Earthquake and tsunami**
Arica
AD 1868

OCEAN

-95

**Earthquake and tsunami**
Chile
AD 1960

stralia
997

**Biggest eruption**
Taupo
BC 700,000

**Earthquake and tsunami**
Talcahuano
AD 1835

45°N

30°N

15°N

0°

15°S

30°S

45°S

165°E   180°   165°W   150°W   135°W   120°W   105°W   90°W   75°W   60°W   45°W

# P R E F A C E

## Pebbles in a stream

We live in a world governed by chance. Events tumble one after the other like pebbles washed down a stream. Some are small, such as the random puff of wind that spreads a dandelion's seeds. Some are big, such as the Big Bang, which got our universe started. Most are in between, such as the movement of continents or the collapse of a civilization. Big and small, important and insignificant, event accumulates on top of event. Eventually, you get history. Occasionally, however, one event creates a cascade of consequences, an avalanche of pebbles. This one event changes everything that follows.

This book is about a select group of natural disasters that had far-reaching consequences with ripple effects across history. A natural disaster is a climatic or environmental occurrence that either kills or injures people, damages property, or causes financial loss. Most are unpredictable, spontaneous calamities called "acts of God." Some, such as fire, may need human help to get started. All of these disasters were crucial shapers of the world we live in.

## A drowned past

Imagine, for example, a world without ancient Greece. No Trojan Wars. No Greek civilization and thus no democracy. No Roman civilization, at least not one based on Greek models. No Roman Republic. No Roman law. No Roman arches, nor domes, nor columns (imagine churches or mosques without them!). No Romance languages. No English language.

That possible present disappeared with the near destruction of Minoan civilization by a volcano and a tsunami. The catastrophe gave the neighboring Mycenaeans their chance for greatness, creating the civilization that would be immortalized in Homer's epic poems about Greece and Troy, *The Iliad* and *The Odyssey*.

I've chosen nine amazing stories, selected for their impact, type, and setting. The events include a blizzard, a typhoon, a hailstorm, an earthquake, a fire, a volcanic eruption, a tsunami, a drought, and an extraterrestrial impact. The final pages are devoted to history-shaping disasters we might experience in the years to come.

## Bigger than us

By focusing on a group of catastrophes selected for their profound effect on human history, I've had to leave a lot out. You'll find no tornadoes here, for example. No landslides, no lightning strikes. Neither Australia (prone to devastating fire and drought) nor South America (cursed with landslides, hurricanes, earthquakes, and tsunamis) is represented. Neither of those continents' disasters have had the kind of documented, long-term ripple effects discussed in these chapters. Moreover, none of the events discussed here are the worst, biggest, or deadliest of their class. If you're a world-record junkie, check out the world map in the front of the book. I've listed a larger cross section of major natural disasters there for context.

It may seem simplistic to make disasters the stars of these historical dramas. What about human ingenuity, personality, culture, politics, technology, and the multitude of other influences that shape history? Surely those are important, too?

True enough. Many factors contributed to these natural disasters and their consequences. But being human, we often overemphasize our role in history: the celebrities, the speeches, the schemes, the romances, and the double-crosses. We're people, and naturally, we find ourselves fascinating. Not so many centuries ago, in fact, we imagined our world as the immobile center of a worshipful universe. The sun, the stars, and all the planets revolved around us: the most important beings in creation.

## An unstable home

Today we know better. Our earth is a small planet with a molten center, a mobile crust, and a thin, unstable atmosphere, bombarded by radiation, hurtling through debris-filled space. We're located at the edge of a large but unexceptional galaxy. Scientists are still counting, but they estimate the universe contains at least 80 billion others.

That we exist at all is by the grace of countless evolutionary accidents. We can think, invent, span continents, dam rivers, and split the atom. We can orbit the globe, visit the moon, communicate across distances instantly, rearrange genes, and manipulate reality. But we're still subject to the same whims of nature as any other species. When disaster strikes—as it does repeatedly and with great effect—it's a reminder of our utter dependence on our dangerous planet for health, wealth, success, power, happiness, and survival.

That's worth remembering.

# Good-bye, Mr. Rex
### How a cosmic impact killed the dinosaurs and gave humanity its chance

65 MILLION B.C.

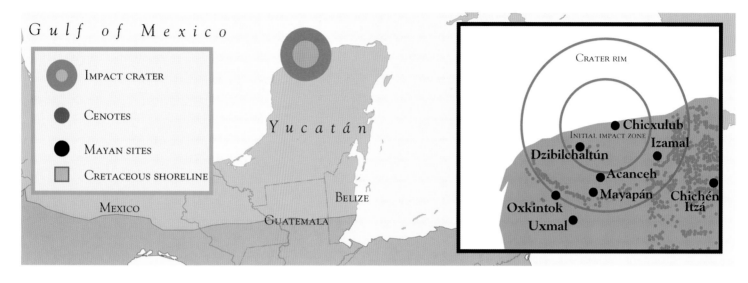

**Gulf of Mexico**

- ⊙ IMPACT CRATER
- ● CENOTES
- ● MAYAN SITES
- ☐ CRETACEOUS SHORELINE

Yucatán

MEXICO

BELIZE

GUATEMALA

CRATER RIM

INITIAL IMPACT ZONE

● Chicxulub

Izamal

Dzibilchaltún

● Acanceh

● Mayapán

Chichén Itzá

Oxkintok

Uxmal

## Extinct again

Since the beginning of life on earth nearly four billion years ago, long periods of gradual evolution have been punctuated by episodes of global mass extinction. Each environmental wipeout has cleared the decks, allowing life to radiate in new directions. The creatures that were dominant before the extinction have been reduced or destroyed. After a pause, new organisms have filled the empty evolutionary niches and grown to dominate the environment. The first of these major extinctions was 440 million years ago. Four more followed at 365, 245, 210, and 65 million years ago. The last mass extinction annihilated the dinosaurs and gave mammals their chance. Mammals begat primates. Primates begat people. An extraterrestrial impact was the probable cause.

## The last big thing

Dinosaurs first appeared 245 million years ago at the beginning of the Triassic Period, a time of warm humidity, lush vegetation, and shallow seas. For the next 180 million years they developed into the crown jewel of evolution. During the Jurassic Period, dinosaurs became the world's dominant species. There were many kinds of dinosaurs all over the earth—and in huge numbers. They died out at the end of the Cretaceous Period, 65 million years ago.

Dinosaurs ranged in size from the tiny to the gigantic. The cat-sized Saltopus was a Triassic Period insect-eater. The earthshaking sauropods like Ultrasaurus, Seismosaurus, and Brachiosaurus were cowlike vegetarians that lived during the late Jurassic and Cretaceous periods. The large theropods like Gigantosaurus, Spinosaurus, and the famous Tyrannosaurus rex were predatory meat-eaters of the Cretaceous Period.

## Crashing the party

We don't know for certain why the dinosaurs vanished. One likely reason, however, was an asteroid or comet that smashed into the earth on what is today Mexico's Yucatán Peninsula. The invader was enormous, perhaps six miles in diameter. It took about a second to traverse our atmosphere and another instant to plow a pit 25 miles deep into the earth's crust. This hole rebounded into a huge mountain of liquefied earth, then collapsed and widened into a crater 90 to 125 miles wide.

The explosion resulting from this impact dramatically changed the environmental conditions that had made dinosaurs so successful. It was equivalent to the detonation of 100 million hydrogen bombs. The heat turned a huge area of the seabed limestone into carbon dioxide, sulfur, and water vapor—"greenhouse gases" that saturated the atmosphere and later, when heated by the sun, could retain more solar heat than the atmosphere before the event. A blast of superheated air swept outward from the impact site, sterilizing the surrounding area for several hundred miles. Molten ejecta from the explosion rained back to earth for several thousand miles. Continent-wide forest fires filled the air with soot. The shock wave pushed the sea into a mile-high

*Even hundreds of miles from the impact site, the blast of superheated air incinerated everything in its path.*

*The explosion resulting from the impact was equivalent to the detonation of 100 million hydrogen bombs.*

tsunami, a giant wave that scoured bare all land within the Caribbean basin and may have deposited sediment as far away as what is now Kansas. This fire and flood left most of North and Central America a lifeless wasteland.

## Hot enough for you?

Dust blasted by the impact into the upper atmosphere eventually encircled the globe, blotting out the sun for months. The planet plunged into a long, cold night. Water vapor returned to earth as acid rain, poisoning the ground and sea. When the dust cleared, the extra carbon dioxide loaded into the atmosphere from the vaporized limestone heated the air to stultifying greenhouse temperatures. This heat may have lasted for a thousand years.

Plants and animals, used to predictable seasonal changes, were unprepared for such radical modifications of their environment; first searing heat, then too-wintry darkness, and finally ultratropical warmth. Half died, never to return. Creatures not killed by the immediate effects of the explosion starved as the food chain collapsed during the Ice Age night. Unable to photosynthesize because sunlight was blocked, plants died. So did the herbivores that fed on them, and the

carnivores that fed on *them*. Other creatures were killed by the acid rain. From tiny zooplankton to gigantic dinosaurs, huge numbers were annihilated—even mighty Tyrannosaurus rex, the king of the dinosaurs.

## Next in line

As in past global extinctions, some life did survive to reproduce, spread, and evolve—otherwise you wouldn't be reading these words. Some bacteria made it, as did turtles, crocodiles, frogs, sharks, and certain plants and mammals. We can only guess why. Some microbes don't need sunlight or oxygen. The seeds and spores of some plants can exist in a dormant state for years until conditions are right for growth. This is also true of the eggs of certain reptiles and amphibians.

Most mammals don't lay eggs. But the mammals of that era were mostly small and furry, which undoubtedly helped them survive both the paucity of food and the initial cold. Some mammals can also hibernate. This may have allowed them to sleep through the worst of the harsh post-catastrophe conditions. When greenhouse temperatures soared, the warm-blooded mammalian ability to regulate body temperature was also a handy feature.

Although large dinosaurs were destroyed by the impact, one dinosaur offshoot possessed the necessary characteristics to cross over: birds. Their small size, feathered insulation, and egg-laying reproduction strategy were the right stuff for the new environment. Birds are sometimes referred to as "avian dinosaurs."

In this new world the survivors spread out and thrived. Over the next several million years, they evolved into a new hierarchy. Birds colonized the air, but also developed into several giant flightless variants, like the thousand-pound elephant bird, which laid eggs as big as basketballs. Mammals metamorphosed from their small and furry progenitors into a class nearly as varied in size and shape as the dinosaurs, from tiny shrews to mighty mastodons. By about 10,000 years ago, however, huge birds and giant mammals had mostly disappeared, possibly affected by climate change or hunted to extinction by the most successful, cunning, ruthless, and adaptable of all animals: people.

## Mystery at the K-T

This story of evolution and extinction wasn't recorded by a camera or written about in a book. It was pieced together by scientists studying the rock record of the history of the earth. The rocks that scientists study for clues are created by sedimentation, the slow deposit over billions of years of eroded rock particles and dead organisms, layer upon layer, at the bottom of lakes, streams, and oceans. Heat and pressure turn these layers into rock. Continental uplift pushes them above water, where we can see them. Changes in the composition of each layer can indicate changes in the environment of that time. Scientists give names to the layers to indicate different time periods.

In the 1980s an international team of scientists led by the geologist Walter Alvarez of the University of California, Berkeley, made discoveries about the K-T boundary. This is the thin layer of sedimentary rock that separates the end of the Cretaceous Period, when the dinosaurs still existed, from the beginning of the Tertiary Period, when they did not.

In between Cretaceous and Tertiary rock is a thin layer of clay that contains iridium. Iridium is an element rare at the earth's surface but common in extraterrestrial objects like meteors. An impact by a meteor or a comet could have spread iridium-bearing dust across the globe.

Once the impact theory was proposed, scientific evidence rapidly accumulated. But the impact crater was hard to find. After years of searching, evidence of the crater was finally discovered near the Mayan village of Chicxulub. Buried beneath layers of younger rock, the crater was detected as an anomaly in the earth's magnetic field.

On the surface of the Yucatán impact zone, the one bit of evidence that can still be seen is a ring of circular holes in the limestone, called *cenotes*, concentrated near its edge. Millions of years after the Chicxulub event, these became the primary source of fresh water for the great Mayan civilization that flourished across the Yucatán in the centuries before the Spanish conquest of the Americas.

## Cosmic roulette

Is an extraterrestrial impact the only explanation for the mass extinctions? No. Some scientists believe volcanoes—another plausible source of the iridium—could have wiped out most Cretaceous life. Others have suggested climate cooling unrelated to an impact or volcanoes. Still others have suggested a global epidemic.

But the impact theory has gained increasing sup-

*Millions of years after the Chicxulub event, the Mayan civilization used the limestone cenotes created by the impact for both fresh water and human sacrifice.*

port. The earth is covered with evidence of other, smaller impacts, and in recent years astronomers have documented several near misses in which comets and asteroids came close to hitting the earth. Recent analysis of the geological record has suggested that the worst of all mass extinctions may have been impact-related. This was the "Great Dying" at the end of the Permian Period, some 245 million years ago. It killed off 90 percent of all life. Nearly all insects were destroyed in that extinction, as were all but two lines of sea urchins. The trilobites, the world's most successful Permian creatures, vanished forever. Two of the survivors were the ancestors of the dinosaurs and, lucky for us, a small, short-legged carnivore—the cynodont—ancestor of all modern mammals.

Where do these cosmic invaders come from? The belt of asteroids orbiting the sun between Mars and Jupiter is one source. Beyond Pluto, however, is the far larger Oort cloud (named after the Dutch astronomer Jan Oort, who first guessed its existence), an immense spherical region of some six trillion comets and other icy objects weakly bound by our sun's gravitational field. Passing stars and other forces can readily change these orbits and send a comet careening into the inner solar system. Luckily, Earth is a small target. Usually, they miss. Chances are, however, that the earth will suffer another major impact and mass extinction within the next 100 million years. Once humanity's ecological niche is empty, who will be the next candidate for global dominance?

# The Tsunami and the Minotaur

*How a giant wave decided the destiny of the West*

1628 B.C.

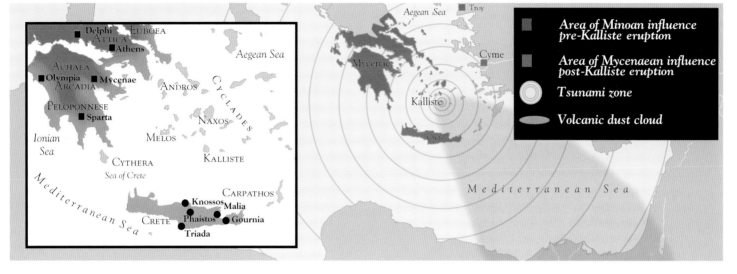

## War and peace

Thirty-six centuries ago a volcanic explosion and a gigantic wave decided which of two brilliant Bronze Age cultures would shape the destiny of Western civilization. The Mycenaeans were a conquering warrior culture based on the Greek mainland. The Minoans were a peaceful maritime people centered on the island of Crete. The volcano blasted the Minoans, the older and more sophisticated of the two, out of history and into myth. The Mycenaeans became the stars of the two most famous poems in Western literature: *The Iliad* and *The Odyssey*.

The first Minoans probably emigrated to Crete from Asia Minor (the western part of present-day Turkey) around 3000 B.C. Some archaeologists suggest that they were the last example of a goddess-worshiping culture that may have once been widespread in Europe and Asia. They were also influenced by the two great civilizations of the day, Egypt and Mesopotamia. By 2100 B.C. the Minoans had developed a distinct culture, centered on the worship of the bull. They spread to other islands in the Aegean Sea, as well as to the Greek mainland and North Africa.

Culturally and technologically, the Minoans were more advanced than anything seen before in Europe. They created two writing systems, neither of which has been deciphered by modern scholars. One was based on hieroglyphic symbols. The other was a syllable-based script. Their refined pottery and metalwork were exported throughout the eastern Mediterranean.

The Minoans became rich on trade. Most lived as well as wealthy aristocrats elsewhere. They built large, multistory stone-and-wood homes with luxurious apartments, reception halls, storerooms, and workshops. Elaborate plumbing included hot and cold running water and flush toilets. Elegant wall paintings depicted birds, flowers, elephants, antelopes, and beautiful women. Meals were prepared in bronze pots and pans that looked remarkably like the cookware of today.

Most amazing of all, Minoan cities lacked fortifications with defensive walls or door locks. The Minoan navy was unrivaled by any neighbor's, and apparently the Minoans lived without fear of invasion. Perhaps the sea was their moat. Imagine: fifteen hundred years of peace.

## Ka-boom!

Around 1628 B.C. the Minoan volcanic island of Kalliste, only 60 miles from Crete, exploded with the force of 150 hydrogen bombs. The eruption pushed Minoan civilization into an abrupt decline. The blast excavated a submarine crater eight miles wide. Some 50 cubic miles of superheated ash and rock shot up into space and out across the sea. On nearby islands

*Throughout the Minoan world, houses were ripped off their foundations by the pounding waves, and ships smashed into kindling in their harbors. Then everything was sucked seaward as the great tide receded.*

such as Naxos, trees were incinerated and people were turned to charcoal by the glowing, blast-furnace air.

The volcanic debris buried Kalliste under thick layers of hot ash, pumice, and stone. Farther away, the spreading volcanic dust cloud cooled from white-hot to red, then to an inky blackness that smothered people and crops. When the explosion was over, what had been Kalliste was a bubbling sulfuric lagoon surrounded by a crater rim of island fragments (the present-day Santorini, consisting of the islands of Thira, Thirasia, and Kameni). Though some inhabitants were killed, many refugees were warned by rumbles and sailed to Crete before the final catastrophe.

## Blue crush

The Kalliste explosion generated enormous ocean waves. These are called *tsunami*, a Japanese word meaning "harbor wave." The term refers to a chain of waves generated by any large disturbance in a body of water. An earthquake, a landslide, a volcanic eruption, an explosion, or even a comet impact can cause a tsunami.

Like the ripples created when a stone is thrown into a pond, tsunamis radiate outward from the point of disturbance. The scale, however, is vastly bigger. On the open sea the passage of a tsunami is nearly imperceptible, just a gradual rise and fall in the ocean surface. As the waves reach shallower water, however, the water piles up and the waves' height grows. When the waves finally reach the coast, they may appear as a rapidly rising or falling tide, a series of breaking waves, or a wall of water. In enclosed seas like the Mediterranean, the distance from the point of disturbance to the shoreline is short, the seabed is shallow, and the potential tsunami height is great. This is particularly true when the rushing water is funneled into narrow fjords and gulfs.

The Kalliste tsunami thrashed the coastlines of Crete, Greece, and even distant Egypt. In parts of Turkey, the waves were 800 feet high and reached 30 miles inland. Throughout the Minoan world, houses were ripped off their foundations by the pounding waves and ships were smashed to kindling in their harbors. Then everything was sucked seaward as the great tide receded.

## There goes the neighborhood

Minoan civilization never recovered. With their fleet maimed, their cities ruined, and their economy stressed by refugees from Kalliste, the Cretans were easy prey for the mainland Mycenaeans, who had been spared the worst effects of the blast. The Mycenaeans invaded Crete and conquered the weakened Minoan society. Mycenaean cities were built atop Minoan ones. Minoan culture was absorbed. Minoan glory receded.

Unlike Minoan culture, Mycenaean culture was based on war and conquest. Mycenaean kings built massive citadels on easily defensible hilltops. Their artisans celebrated kingly power with giant tombs, gorgeous wall decorations, and magnificent gold ornaments. They also produced fine pottery, metalwork, stone vessels, and ivory carvings that were traded throughout the eastern Mediterranean. They fielded armies equipped with horse-drawn chariots, bows and arrows, bronze armor, shields, and spears. Their writing is an early form of Greek. Their gods were the forerunners of the Greek divinities of the later classical period.

## You're history

After the explosion of Kalliste, the Mycenaeans had a 500-year run as a major Mediterranean power. But in the twelfth century B.C., invading Dorian armies conquered the Mycenaeans, plunging Greece into a 400-year dark age. By the time of the founding of the Olympics in 776 B.C., a new Greek culture had begun to emerge, unified by a new alphabet and literature. It matured in the fifth century B.C., Greece's classical age. The classical Greeks developed theories of democracy, science, mathematics, philosophy, architecture, religion, theater, and poetry that are the basis of Western culture today. They also gave us a society dominated by men, based on conquest, and supported by slaves. In the fourth century B.C. these ideas—Hellenistic civilization—were spread by the Macedonian conqueror Alexander the Great from the Aegean to Egypt through Afghanistan to India. In India, Greco-Roman art mixed with indigenous forms; as the classical Indian Gupta style, it spread to China, Japan, and Southeast Asia. After Greece was taken over by the Romans, Greek ideas were transmitted throughout Europe and by the Europeans to America.

The two most famous works of ancient Western literature come from eighth-century B.C. Greece but describe the earlier Mycenaean world. These are the poet Homer's *Iliad* and *Odyssey*. These epics immortalize Greek warrior culture by recounting the Mycenaean conquest of Troy, an Asia Minor city-state. They continue to influence contemporary Western literature, politics, technology, movies, sports, and war. The English language is filled with Homeric phrases (Trojan horse, Achilles' heel), place names (Ithaca, Troy), and personalities (Circe, Calypso, Cyclops). Our planets are named after the Roman versions of the Homeric gods.

## Greek bedtime stories

And the Minoans? They were reduced to bit players in the Greek saga. In myth, their entire culture was reduced to a single island, guarded by Talos, a gigantic brass man. It was ruled by King Minos (from whom Minoan culture gets its name). In Minos' palace, Greek youths were sacrificed in the maze of the Labyrinth to the bull-headed Minotaur, a monster who was finally destroyed by the Greek hero Theseus. King Minos also imprisoned the inventor Daedalus and his son, Icarus. Their escape on homemade wax-and-feather wings was ruined when the impetuous Icarus flew too near the sun, melted the wax, lost his feathers, and fell to his death in the sea.

The Minoan disaster may have inspired one more piece of Greek literature. In 347 B.C. the Greek philosopher Plato retold an old Egyptian story about an ancient continent-sized utopia called Atlantis, which in the distant past was swallowed up "in a single day and night." This most famous of lost civilizations has inspired generations of would-be discoverers, multitudes of knock-off stories, and even a Disney animated movie. But not a shred of Atlantean evidence has ever been found. Intriguingly, Plato's lost continent suggests the religion, architecture, and many of the customs of the Minoan world. Could Atlantis be Kalliste or even Crete?

It could be.

*In classical Greek literature, Minoan civilization was reduced to a single island, guarded by Talos, a gigantic brass man.*

# Wet Blessing, Dry Curse

*How an African empire died of thirst*

## A temporary superpower

Travel less than a hundred miles from the desert shores of the Red Sea to the high Ethiopian Plateau and you'll see them: the dusty, broken remnants of a great kingdom. Shattered monuments, looted tombs, empty courtyards, and the bare foundations of grand homes rest on hilly plains scarred by deep erosion channels. This is Aksum, a cautionary tale of power and wealth, raised high and laid low in part by a shift in climate. It is a disaster story that took place not in seconds, minutes, or even hours, but over centuries.

From the first to the eighth centuries A.D., Aksum was sub-Saharan Africa's most important civilization. At the kingdom's height in the fourth and fifth centuries, Aksum's territory extended across the southern periphery of the Roman empire from the Sahara to the inner Arabian Desert. To its Mediterranean contemporaries, Aksum was considered one of the known world's four great powers, along with Rome, Persia, and China. Although smaller and less populous than those rivals, Aksum was a critical supplier of raw materials. It controlled most of the trade between the outside world and the African hinterland. A large part of the empire's importance was due to a happy coincidence of location and climate.

## Location, location, location

The Ethiopian Plateau is a curious place for the capital of a trading empire. The Plateau is located on the Horn of Africa at the edge of the Sahel, the continental swath of arid plain south of the Sahara Desert. The Plateau is isolated from the surrounding environment not only by its height—an average of 6,500 feet above sea level—but also by successive ranks of steep, high cliffs. Travel on the Plateau proper is hindered by ranges of snowcapped mountains and deep chasms like the Great Rift Valley, the Tekeze gorge, the canyon of the Blue Nile River, and the Danakil depression, one of the lowest places in Africa.

But Aksum's situation had advantages. Although Aksum was located near the equator, the Plateau's high altitude gave it the benefit of a temperate climate. It was cooler and wetter than the heat-blasted deserts and scrubland to the east and west. It was free of the tropical diseases that plagued the dank equatorial jungles to the south. Moreover, Aksum benefited from the Plateau's many unique food plants: the cereal grain *teff*, the oil-producing *noog* (the "Niger seed"), *ensete* (the "false banana"), and most important for later civilizations, coffee.

Although secluded, Aksum was close enough to the Red Sea to benefit from the considerable trade that flowed between the Eastern Roman empire and civilizations around the Indian Ocean. The Red Sea port of Adulis—eight days' march from Aksum through what today is Eritrea—was the kingdom's gateway to international trade. Through Adulis, Aksum exported ivory, rhinoceros horn, hippopotamus hides, salt, human slaves, civet cat musk, live elephants, ebony, gold dust, and frankincense, among other goods. Frankincense in particular was a source of enormous wealth for the empire. An aromatic resin burned by the ton throughout the Mediterranean as religious

By the end of the rainy years, Aksum's eroded, overworked soil could not grow enough food to feed its people. When drought came, famine and population collapse followed.

incense and used to treat ailments from stomach ache to cancer, frankincense was produced by a tree that grew almost entirely within the boundaries of the Aksumite empire. Thousands of tons were produced annually. It was as highly prized as gold.

## Babies and bumper crops

From the first to the eighth centuries A.D., Aksum got lucky. The climate became cooler and wetter. Monsoon rains that normally fall south of Ethiopia moved north. Added onto the Plateau's usual rains, the monsoon extended the time during which farmers could grow crops from three months to six or even nine. Aksumite farmers who could usually grow only one crop a year now got two. With more available food, the population grew. By A.D. 500 Aksum proper covered about a quarter square mile and housed some 20,000 inhabitants. (By comparison, at the same time, Rome boasted about a million inhabitants living in an area of five square miles.) Aksum's rulers raised armies, invaded and enslaved their neighbors, and expanded their territory. They took to wearing multi-pointed, jeweled crowns that got bigger and gaudier with each new kingly generation. They imported luxury items that fed the growing appetites of the ruling classes: fine glassware and ceramics, precious metals, fancy textiles, wine, sugarcane, and spices.

With more labor, Aksum's kings were able to command bigger palaces and monuments. They commissioned stone memorials, commemorating their conquests. They marked their tombs with tower-like monuments decorated with idealized representations of their multi-storied wooden homes. The biggest monument, over 100 feet high, depicts a 13-story house (real ones were probably only three stories). It weighed 700 tons, the largest piece of stone quarried in human history. It now lies broken where it fell, shattered into five enormous chunks.

To facilitate trade and underscore the empire's growing power, Aksum issued coinage—the first African kingdom to do so—in gold, silver, and bronze. The coinage was based on Roman weights and measures, but featured portraits of the Aksumite kings. Inscriptions were written in Greek and Ge'ez, the kingdom's writing system. (The forerunner of Amharic, the modern language of Ethiopia, Ge'ez is sub-Saharan Africa's only indigenous script.) The coins circulated throughout the Mediterranean and have been found as far away as India.

## Nothing is permanent

By the fourth century A.D. Aksum was at its peak, but new forces—political and environmental—would soon undercut the basis of the empire's power. The Mediterranean was entering a period of increasing political instability, and the Horn of Africa was about to experience another round of abrupt climate change.

Until the fourth century the Aksumites were pagans, worshiping a pantheon of gods similar to those of pre-Islamic South Arabia. But, following Rome's lead, Aksum adopted Christianity as the state religion. The strategic move may have helped consolidate the kingdom's position as a valuable ally on the Roman empire's southern flank. With the fall of the Western Roman empire in the fifth century, however, and the increasing impoverishment of the Eastern Roman empire in the late sixth and early seventh centuries, the market for Aksumite goods shrank. Trade with India dried up when Sassanian Persians gained control of South Arabia. Finally, with the birth of Islam in the seventh century and consequent unification of Arabia, the Mediterranean's political balance of power was changed utterly. Initially, Aksum was a critical Islamic ally, but in the early eighth century, Arab forces destroyed Adulis, cutting off Aksum from its principal port.

Even without political catastrophe, Aksum's destruction was assured by environmental degradation. The long centuries of extended rainy seasons had encouraged expanded farming and woodcutting. By the sixth century those practices had stripped all but Aksum's steepest hillsides and deepest gorges of woodland cover. The long rains leached out nutrients, washed away topsoil, and caused severe erosion. Crop yields dropped. The population began to starve. By the seventh century Aksum had been reduced to village clusters. The ruling classes moved from their flatland palaces to defensible hilltops, protecting their privileges to the end.

Then, around A.D. 750, rainfall patterns on the Ethiopian Plateau returned to the shorter norm of a single three-month growing season. Agricultural production on the eroded, impoverished soil plummeted. Because of too much then not enough rain, the once mighty superpower was forced to its knees. Centralized power collapsed. Aksum was abandoned. It vanished from the outside world's attention until archaeological excavation in the nineteenth century led to its rediscovery.

The climatic fluctuations that Aksum experienced,

*To satisfy the need for more timber, more charcoal, and more food, Aksum cut down all but its most inaccessible forests.*

dry to wet to dry again, had several causes. Over the long term—a 22,000-year cycle—the tilt of the earth's rotation cools the planet and locks up water in the polar glaciers. In Africa this makes the desert and Sahel regions drier, reducing vegetation and reflecting more of the sun's radiation back into space. In the short term, changes in temperature, vegetation, wind, and rain cause droughts that can be local, regional, or continental. The El Niño Southern Oscillation (ENSO) may be one factor affecting African rainfall. *El Niño* is a term used to describe a periodic warming of the surface of the eastern tropical Pacific Ocean, followed by a cooling called *La Niña*. This seesaw change in temperature causes chain reactions in rainfall worldwide. In Africa it abbreviates or extends seasonal rains like the monsoon.

## Glory days

Aksum was the last purely African civilization able to maneuver internationally on a par with the great empires of Europe and Asia. The empire's collapse foreshadowed centuries of African exploitation by outside powers in the emerging world order. First the Arab world, then Europe, then the Americas proceeded to mine Africa for the continent's raw materials: gold, gems, timber, animals, oil, but especially and most disgracefully, human beings. Over the centuries, at least 20 million people were exported from Africa, to work and die as slaves.

Today Aksum is only a shadow, but an important shadow. In the thirteenth century a new line of Christian kings emerged in central Ethiopia. To confer legitimacy on their new lineage, these Ethiopian rulers invented an impressive patrimony linked to Aksum. They traced their origins back to a mythical first Aksumite king called Menelik. They said he was the son of King Solomon and the Queen of Sheba. They credited him with bringing the sacred Ark of the Covenant from Jerusalem to Aksum. According to the Bible, the Ark is the repository of the stone tablets on which God wrote the Ten Commandments. The Bible says the Ark disappeared, but is silent on its ultimate fate.

Ethiopia's "Solomonic dynasty" ended in 1974, when the 111th emperor in line from Solomon, Haile Selassie, was deposed in a military coup. But to this day Ethiopian tradition still holds that the Ark can be found in Aksum's Cathedral of Mary of Zion. A replica of the Ark—a *tabot*—is kept in every Ethiopian Orthodox church. It is a last link, however tenuous, to Ethiopia's glory days, when climate smiled on the Horn of Africa.

# Kamikaze-ing Kublai Khan

*How two storms saved Japan from Mongolian conquest*

A.D. 1274

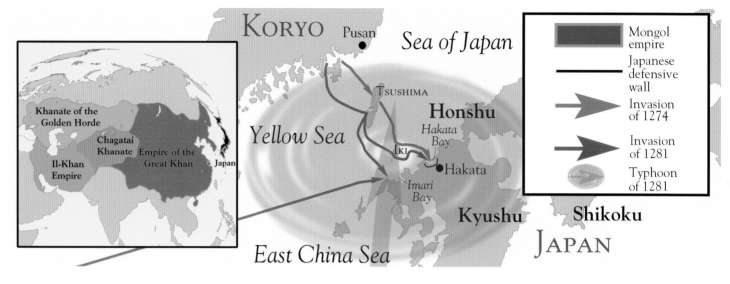

## The bully next door

In 1268 the emperor of China sent envoys to the emperor of Japan offering a stark choice: subservience or war. It was occasion for careful consideration. Japan was an island nation, proud, independent, and never conquered. But China's emperor was Kublai Khan, leader of the Mongol empire. The Mongols had already conquered four-fifths of Asia, from Korea to the Polish frontier. Every major city in Korea had been sacked. Some 40 million Chinese had been killed, nearly half the country's population. The skulls of the defeated were piled into huge roadside pyramids. Unless the Japanese agreed to pay tribute, they would likely suffer the same fate.

On the other hand, all those Mongol conquests had been on land. Japan is a small series of islands in the Pacific Ocean. Though ferocious, the Mongols had no experience with amphibious invasion. So the Japanese stalled. They considered all manner of tactful refusals. Finally they sent the khan's emissaries home empty-handed and waited for the worst. No one knew that weather, not warriors, would decide the outcome of Japan's battle for survival.

In response to this Japanese impertinence, Kublai Khan created the Office for the Conquest of the East. More than 35,000 men in Koryo, his Korean vassal state, were forced to build a fleet of 900 ships. An invasion force of 40,000 Mongol cavalry, Chinese infantry, Korean sailors, and support troops was assembled to attack Japan.

In October 1274 the invaders crossed the Tsushima Strait from Korea. They occupied the Japanese island of Tsushima, then Iki, massacring the garrisons. On November 19 they arrived at Kyushu, Japan's main southern island. They landed at Hakata Bay, where they were met by the Japanese defenders.

The Mongol warriors overwhelmed the Japanese. The samurai (Japanese knights) expected warrior-to-warrior single combat. They had no experience with Mongol artillery barrages (catapults armed with smoking gunpowder balls, flaming arrows, and rocks) and massed cavalry charges. By dusk, the Japanese had been pushed miles inland to Hakata's ancient stone fortifications. But instead of pressing their advantage, the Mongols decided to return to their ships for the evening. We don't know why. This was storm season and the weather was worsening. The worried Korean captains may have convinced the Mongols to go to their ships for safety.

## Think it'll rain?

The tempest that struck a few hours later was extraordinarily fierce. Many Mongol ships that made for open sea foundered, smashed into one another, or were driven onto rocks. When the gale passed, 200 ships had been destroyed and 13,000 warriors had drowned. The surviving fleet limped home. The next morning, the Japanese were amazed to find the Mongols completely gone.

The Japanese called the storm that overcame the invader *kamikaze*, the divine wind. In fact, the storm was a tropical cyclone. These occur in every ocean north and south of the equator between 5 and 20

One hundred thousand invaders died in the typhoon of 1281. Accounts from the aftermath indicate that in Imari Bay, "a person could walk across from one point of land to another on a mass of wreckage."

degrees latitude, during summer and fall. They affect every continent except Antarctica and have many regional names. Australians sometimes call them willy-willies, though elsewhere in the Southern Hemisphere and the Indian Ocean they are called cyclones. In the Caribbean, the Atlantic, and the North Pacific they are called hurricanes (from *huracán*, the Taino Indian word for "evil spirit"). In the eastern Pacific they are called typhoons (from *ta feng*, a Chinese expression meaning "violent wind").

Tropical cyclones result from the convergence of several climatic trends, starting with the midsummer heating of tropical oceans. This makes the thunderstorms that occur over these waters rise; in turn, atmospheric pressure drops, and this draws in the trade winds. With proper conditions in place, these air currents rotate ever faster, sucking energy from the ocean surface.

Conversely, in the center of this disturbance—the eye of the storm—dry air is forced down from high altitudes. This creates a calm, cloudless nucleus that is eventually surrounded by a spinning wall of towering thunderheads. As the storm builds, atmospheric pressure continues to drop, pulling in even faster winds over a larger area. It's a self-perpetuating cycle fed by the transfer of energy from the water to the air. The storm dissipates only when it hits cooler water, or land.

Tropical cyclones are tremendously destructive. They can be 600 miles across with speeds of 200 miles per hour. This is powerful enough to ram pine needles into bark and to destroy most human-made structures. The lowered atmospheric pressure can raise the ocean surface into a storm surge, a hill of water that moves forward with the storm. At sea, this oceanic battering ram can grow into wind-driven waves 25 feet high, even higher in enclosed bays. On shore, the storm surge can rush inland far past the high-tide line.

## Surrender—or else

We don't know if the Mongol withdrawal in 1274 was a planned or a storm-induced defeat. We do know that by 1279 Kublai Khan had sent another diplomatic mission to Japan. This time he demanded that the Japanese emperor present himself at the Mongol capital to answer for his actions. Alarmed, the Japanese beheaded the unfortunate emissaries upon their arrival in Kyoto.

When word of this outrage reached the khan, he established the Office for the Chastisement of Japan. He ordered an even bigger invasion fleet. Exactly how big we don't know for sure, but there were at least 900 more ships from Koryo to carry 40,000 Mongol, Korean, and northern Chinese troops, plus 600 ships from southern China to carry 100,000 Chinese soldiers (apparently, they built ships bigger in China than in Korea).

Preparations complete, Kublai Khan sent more envoys. This time the Japanese didn't even let the emissaries reach Kyoto. They were beheaded on the beach. In March 1281 the northern Mongol fleet set sail for Kyushu.

The Japanese had been doing more than decapitating Chinese ambassadors, though. They knew their survival was at stake. For defense, they built a shoreline wall at Hakata 15 feet high and 25 miles long. They set up defensive positions at most principal harbors on the coast facing Korea. Strategic roads were improved. A small fleet of ships was constructed. Local defense forces were reorganized. New draftees

brought Kyushu's fighting strength up to 100,000 men. Battle tactics were modified so the samurai could fight in groups. Meanwhile, Buddhist and Shinto priests prayed for a second kamikaze.

The northern fleet arrived first, attacking Tsushima and Iki islands as well as the Shiga peninsula in Hakata Bay. By June the southern fleet had begun arriving at various points west and south of Hakata. This time, the Japanese successfully resisted. The fighting continued through July, with heavy losses on both sides. The Mongols were able to gain only coastal beachheads. Meanwhile, the tiny Japanese fleet managed a hit-and-run campaign, harrying and setting fire to Mongol ships.

## Rain? Again?

On August 15, 1281, in one of history's biggest repeat ironies, a full-blown typhoon arrived. Again the khan's ships were smashed to pieces. Almost the entire fleet was destroyed. Accounts from the aftermath indicate that in Imari Bay, "a person could walk across from one point of land to another on a mass of wreckage." One hundred thousand invaders died.

Kublai Khan's defeat broke Mongol strength in China, though it took nearly a century for the dynasty to collapse. A third invasion was ordered, then rescinded. Invasions of Indochina and Indonesia also failed. No longer invincible, Kublai had to raise taxes and demand extra labor from the peasants to pay for the failed invasions. Finally, in 1294, Kublai Khan died. Nine short-lived successors followed. Then the peasants revolted and the Mongols were thrown out. In 1368 a new Chinese dynasty was founded—the Ming.

In Japan the results of the Mongol defeat resonated for centuries. Traditionally, samurai expected captured land and booty as rewards for their valor. But because the Japanese were defending their own turf, the usual spoils of war were not forthcoming. This upset both the feudal barons who had done the fighting and the Buddhist and Shinto priests who believed their prayers had caused the divine wind. Unable to contain the discontent, the government collapsed, ushering in two centuries of turbulence. This unrest paradoxically produced many of the famously refined Japanese cultural traditions: Noh theater, the tea ceremony, sumi-e ink painting, ikebana flower arranging, and landscape gardening.

## Death and rebirth

The legend of the kamikaze winds grew into a sense of Japanese national invincibility that persisted for centuries. During the Second World War, Japan's new military dictatorship tried to draw on the country's ancient triumph over the Mongols by creating a new kind of kamikaze: suicide fighter pilots who crashed their planes into Allied warships. These very mortal divine winds did a great deal of damage but ultimately failed to prevent Japan's eventual surrender and occupation by the Allies. The Japan that emerged from that defeat was a new nation, no longer a militaristic power, but a democratic, constitutional monarchy. In this Japan the will of the people, not the divine winds, rules the land.

*Japanese samurai were used to knightly single combat, where each warrior called out a ritual challenge and recited his personal history before battle. These rituals proved ineffective against Mongol massed-cavalry charges. Nor did they work against the Mongol artillery: clouds of smoking gunpowder balls, rocks, flaming and poisoned arrows, shot from catapults.*

# Hail to the King

*How ice saved France from an English monarch*

A.D. 1360

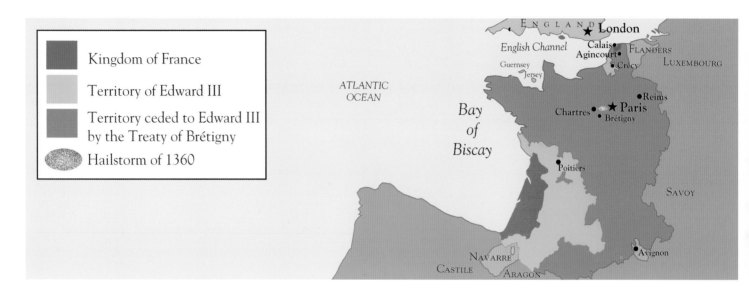

Kingdom of France

Territory of Edward III

Territory ceded to Edward III by the Treaty of Brétigny

Hailstorm of 1360

## Mr. Congeniality

When King Edward III of England claimed the crown of France, he wasn't expecting to start the Hundred Years' War. It might have ended sooner, and differently, if not for a hailstorm.

Since the Norman conquest of England in 1066, the French and English monarchies had been closely related. French was the language of the English court. Through inheritance, the English already controlled a portion of the French mainland.

When the French ruler Charles IV died without a male heir in 1328, a cousin, Philip de Valois, succeeded him. England's Edward—whose mother was sister to three French kings—asserted a competing claim.

The French couldn't bear the idea of an English ruler. They rejected Edward with the excuse that he could not inherit the crown through the female line. In 1337 Edward sent a letter of defiance to "Pilip [sic] of Valois, who calls himself king of France." In 1340 Edward assumed the title "king of England and France."

Edward's desire to rule France was not just ego. Fourteenth-century England and France were bitter rivals. France was the wealthiest country in Europe and the most populous, with 20 million inhabitants to England's 5 million. England, however, had a stronger central government, a more battle-hardened army, a thriving economy, and, in Edward, a popular king. If Edward controlled France, he would expand England's already substantial land holdings on the Continent and safeguard his country's principal source of foreign trade: wool.

## Wine in sheep's clothing

The English economy of that era depended on a triangle of trade. English fleece was shipped across the Channel to France's northern neighbor, Flanders, where it was woven into woolen cloth. The cloth was exchanged for wine in the grape-producing land England controlled in southern France. The wine was shipped back across the Channel to England, where it was consumed by the upper class (peasants drank beer). From 1337 to 1453 England and France fought over control of the Channel, over Flanders, and over England's Continental possessions. This was the Hundred Years' War.

When the French tried to assert control of Flanders, Edward acted. In 1340 his navy totally destroyed the French fleet, giving the English control of the Channel. Edward could now attack France without fear of their reprisal on the home island. By 1345 Edward had raised an army of noble knights, peasant soldiers, and mercenaries. They invaded the French mainland and, for the next fifteen years, ravaged the French countryside, looting and wrecking towns.

*An apocalyptic storm of hailstones the size of pigeon eggs pummeled Edward's army, electrocuting knights in their armor, shredding tents, and smashing luggage wagons. Hundreds of men and horses died.*

*When the Duke of Lancaster's hail-battered armor was removed, his chain mail left bloody indentations on his skin.*

The English repeatedly outmatched the French forces sent against them. In 1346 they won the battle of Crécy. In 1356 they had a spectacular victory at Poitiers. There they captured the French king (no longer Philip, but his son and successor, Jean II). By November 1359, the English army was marching toward Reims, the city where French monarchs traditionally were crowned. At last Edward III, Europe's most successful warrior, seemed poised to become king of France.

## Black Monday

Then Edward's fortunes turned. English soldiers lived partially off the land. But the land, wrecked by years of pillage, yielded neither enough food for the English troops nor food for their horses. The winter weather became brutal. Starvation loomed.

Moreover, Edward's enemies refused to emerge from their newly fortified cities. Under such conditions, laying siege was arduous. Reims resisted all that winter. An Easter campaign to capture Paris also foundered.

Then came Black Monday. On April 13, 1360, while Edward's soldiers marched toward Chartres, the skies went dark. The air became bitterly cold. The heavens opened, and an apocalyptic storm sent hail-

stones the size of pigeon eggs smashing into Edward's army. Tents were shredded. Luggage carts were swept away. Lightning electrocuted knights in their armor. Hundreds of men and more than a thousand horses died. When the storm ended, what was left of Edward's army limped into the tiny village of Brétigny, where monks sheltered the survivors and attended to their considerable wounds. Meanwhile, Edward pondered the meaning of this icy catastrophe.

## Just ice

Hail is ice. It is formed by the repeated freezing of supercooled droplets of water lifted by the air currents of thunderstorms. Though the rare giant hailstone has been reported (one that fell in India was allegedly as big as an elephant), hail usually ranges from tiny soft particles called graupel to baseball-sized chunks.

To form, hail needs below-freezing temperatures and a nucleus—some material center around which the hail can build. Usually the hail nucleus is a speck of airborne dust. Occasionally, however, living creatures suffer this fate. Insects and birds caught in storms have been turned into hail nuclei, as have frogs, turtles, and fish sucked up by tornadoes and waterspouts. One case of human hailstones occurred in 1930 over Germany when five glider pilots bailed out into a thunderstorm. Carried up and down through the updrafts and downdrafts, the nucleus—dust, animal, or human—is coated and recoated with ice.

Eventually it is too heavy to be supported by air currents and falls to earth.

Hail is usually short-lived and affects only a limited area, damaging rather than killing. But occasionally it falls by the ton: for example, in 1968, a single 90-minute hailstorm over Illinois produced 84 million cubic feet of ice. The power of Edward's hail encounter can be glimpsed by the marks it left on one of his heavily armored knights, the Duke of Lancaster. When the chain mail was removed from this wounded nobleman, the iron rings had been pressed into his skin, leaving bloody indentations. Foot soldiers fared far worse. They wore only leather caps and padded clothing to protect themselves. They were simply pounded to death.

## A *really* big hint

The fourteenth century was an age of superstition, when natural events were perceived as signs from God. Edward had already experienced the Black Death (bubonic plague) of 1348–51. That calamity and its aftermath killed a third of Europe's population, making the end of the world a vivid possibility. The Black Monday catastrophe—a drubbing delivered not by the French but the heavens—was reason for pause. Was it a sign to give up the quest for the French crown, or just bad luck?

No record of Edward's interpretation survives, and historians differ in their analyses of his actions following the storm. But his next steps are telling. Three weeks after Edward's diminished army arrived in Brétigny, Edward agreed to a truce. He got a third of France and a huge ransom for the return of Jean II. He gave up his claim to the French crown.

*His ambitions for the domination of France smashed, Edward and what was left of his army sailed home to England. But the Hundred Years' War would drag on for many more weary decades.*

Both sides soon recanted these concessions, and battles started afresh. Although the Hundred Years' War was just beginning, the real turning point had already been reached. The Black Monday hailstorm marked the end of Edward's successes in France. Over the next twenty years, the French, by force and bribery, reversed Edward's territorial gains. Despite later victories by Edward's descendants (the English win at the battle of Agincourt is the most famous), none managed to become king of France, though they kept trying for many weary decades.

## Leggo my island

The Hundred Years' War helped undo both the feudal knight and the medieval social order. Hail was the least of many superior enemies. Knightly traditions of chivalry, glory, and single combat were ineffective against new technologies like the longbow and firearms, wielded by commoners. Eventually, ad hoc companies of peasants led by armored knights on horseback were replaced by professional standing armies. The modern state evolved to maintain them.

After the Hundred Years' War, the English began to emphasize sea power. This resulted, centuries later, in the globe-spanning British Empire. But they did not give up their claims to the French mainland. Only in 1565 were the English finally forced out of Calais, their last foothold in Continental France. Only in 1801 did they remove the French fleur-de-lis from the royal coat of arms, after the French Revolution—and the guillotine—had removed the head of the last hereditary French monarch. Today England still controls the two tiny Channel Islands, Jersey and Guernsey—the last remnants of its medieval empire in France.

# It Started on Pudding Lane

### How cities were remade after the Great Fire of London

A.D. 1666

## Whoops

We can thank Thomas Farynor for the proliferation of brick and stone buildings in modern cities. Also for gridded streets and municipal fire departments. Fire insurance, too. None of these innovations were his idea, just his fault.

Thomas Farynor was baker to King Charles II. On the night of September 2, 1666, someone in his bakery on Pudding Lane forgot to douse the embers before going to bed. It might have been Farynor himself, a baker's assistant, a maid, or another servant. Whoever erred, within a few hours that mistake set the bakery alight. Over the next four days, nearly all of London burned.

London had suffered repeated fires since its founding in Roman times. But systematic efforts at fire prevention did not occur until the eleventh century, when William the Conqueror's *couvre-feu* (origin of the word *curfew*) prescribed the covering of all cooking fires and lights at nightfall. Later rulers added their own innovations. As of 1583 candlemakers were no longer allowed to melt tallow, a highly flammable substance used to make candles, in their dwellings. In 1647 wooden chimneys were banned.

But Thomas Farynor's London was still a medieval city. Streets were narrow and winding. Buildings were closely packed and most construction was "half-timbered," with wooden-framework walls filled in with plaster. Roofs were made of thatch (straw and leaves) and sealed with pitch, a sticky substance derived from wood and coal. Bakery ovens were constructed from wickerwork basketry or brick and coated with clay. Wood was used for both oven doors and fuel. Candles and lamps provided evening light.

Under these circumstances, accidental fires were a constant danger and a common occurrence. Thomas Farynor's misfortune was to start his accidental fire on a windy night at the end of a long hot summer. The city was tinder dry. Drought had depleted water reserves. Only a spark was needed to start an unstoppable conflagration.

## You *must* try the rat flambé

The fire spread from Pudding Lane down Fish Street Hill to the warehouses and wharves of Thames Street. There the flames fed on the stores of hay, timber, coal, tallow, brandy, oil, and hemp. Engorged with these combustibles, the fire became too fierce for the primary defense of the day: bucket brigades. These volunteers tried to put out fires by dousing them with pail after pail of water, passed hand to hand from a water source to the blaze. In this case, the water was supposed to come from the Thames River. That supply was cut off when the fire burned the waterwheel at London Bridge, the only reliable way to move large quantities of water from the river to street level.

*Seventeenth-century London was still a medieval city. Buildings were closely packed, half-timbered, and pitch-roofed, easy prey to fire. When the spark came from the bakery on Pudding Lane, the flames quickly spread, pushed by an east wind.*

*Metal firemarks were used by the first English insurance company fire brigades to identify homes that they insured. This firemark depicted the mythical phoenix, a bird that is burned, then reborn from flames. Sometimes, burning homes without a firemark were ignored.*

Fanned by an east wind, the fire spread into the heart of the city, threatening the wealthy area of Cornhill. The indecisive Lord Mayor Bludworth hesitated to authorize the next preventative measure, depriving the fire of fuel by demolishing the fashionable homes now in its path. So the flames continued to spread, engulfing the famous St. Paul's Cathedral. The heat caused the lead seams of the church's roof to run in streams and the stones of the walls to explode like grenades. Refugees streamed from the city, carrying what they could into the Thames and out of the city to the surrounding countryside.

Eventually King Charles himself ordered firebreaks. Buildings were pulled down with poles, ladders, and axes or blown up with gunpowder. Finally, on the fourth day of the blaze, the wind died and the fire was contained. Four-fifths of the city had been destroyed, an area of about one and a half square miles. Gone were 13,200 homes, 44 guild halls, and 84 parish churches, a degree of devastation not seen again in London until the Blitz of World War II. Some 100,000 people were made homeless. Astonishingly, by official counts, only four people died.

Yet there was some benefit. The Great Fire ended an epidemic of bubonic plague that had begun the previous year and killed 68,000 people. The flames had incinerated the city's plentiful rat population, whose fleas had been the primary carriers of the plague.

## Ambulance chaser

Only days after the flames were extinguished, architect Christopher Wren presented a plan to King Charles to rebuild the entire city along classical lines. His design also called for broad, tree-lined streets cutting through the old warren of twisting lanes and alleys. That idea was rejected, but Wren was appointed to supervise the rebuilding of the city's churches. Over the next 46 years he designed 51 of them, all different, all inspired by the columns, domes, symmetrical lines, and beautiful proportions of classical Greco-Roman architecture. His masterpiece was a rebuilt St. Paul's, which exists to this day. These structures significantly changed London's appearance, creating a grander, more imperial city. Justifiably, Wren is considered England's most brilliant architect.

Christopher Wren also designed the Monument, a tall column near Pudding Lane commemorating the Great Fire. Bakers hated it. A trial (with three Farynors on the jury) blamed foreign plotters. Robert Hubert, a mentally unstable French watchmaker, confessed. Despite conflicting evidence, he was convicted and hanged. Only in 1986 did London's bakers' guild, the Worshipful Company of Bakers, finally apologize.

## Got insurance?

The Rebuilding Act of 1667 was London's first comprehensive building code. It regulated the height of all secular buildings and allowed only four types of houses, all of brick or stone. Streets were widened to create potential firebreaks. New firefighting devices were invented, like an early fire engine. This was a wooden tub equipped with carrying handles, a pump, and a small hose, which was supplied with water by a bucket brigade.

The Great Fire ruined thousands of Londoners financially. The fortunate had savings or inherited wealth or could borrow money to rebuild their homes and businesses. Most others ended up in debtors' prison, that era's solution to those who couldn't pay their bills. For future victims, financial catastrophe was averted through the invention of fire insurance. Individuals who wanted to be prepared for devastating fire loss could pay an annual premium to an insurance company. It pooled the funds of all insured members and paid them out to fire victims whose property was destroyed.

The insurance companies realized that if there were fewer fires they would pay fewer claims and realize higher profits. So they organized private fire brigades. Insured buildings were identified by a metal "firemark" affixed to the outside. But private brigades tended to let structures burn if they bore a competitor's mark. The companies were eventually combined into a municipal force, the London Fire Engine Establishment.

## Penntopia

Although Christopher Wren's London redesign was rejected, Richard Newcourt's unrealized plans for rebuilding the city may have inspired William Penn, the founder of Philadelphia. Penn lived through both the Plague of 1665 and the Great Fire of 1666. He wanted a city that would be fire-resistant and disease-free, or as he put it, "never be burnt and always be wholesome." Penn designed a grid of 100-foot-wide streets for Philadelphia, the broadest of their day. Penn's town core was surrounded by 80-acre gentlemen's estates whose mansions were to be at least 800 feet apart and surrounded by fields and gardens. This ring was surrounded by a greenbelt. Though Philadelphia has expanded beyond those original limits, the broad outlines of William Penn's expansive "green towne" still survive in the city's core.

## Note to self: wood still burns

Although Philadelphia-style city grids, broad streets, stone and brick buildings, and fire insurance are now present in most modern cities around the world, it took years, decades—even centuries in some places—for the ideas to catch on. Usually, it took a catastrophic fire.

Like seventeenth-century London, nineteenth-century Chicago was built almost entirely of wood. The city was growing fast. Forests were still plentiful. Wood was the cheapest available building material.

Tens of thousands of buildings were made of wood. Fifty-seven of Chicago's 450 miles of streets were paved with wood. Some 561 miles of wooden sidewalks edged them. Sawmills and factories were stacked high with raw logs and wooden inventory.

On October 8, 1871, it all burned.

As in London, the Great Chicago Fire started at night, at the end of a long hot summer. As in London, the fire was driven by a strong wind. As in London, firefighting equipment was inadequate. This Great Fire killed at least 250 people and left 100,000 homeless. Nearly 18,000 structures were destroyed in a two-by-four-mile area. Some $200 million in property was damaged, about a third of the city's entire value (and about $2.7 billion in today's dollars). Although about half of this was insured, the scale of the catastrophe forced many of the fire-insurance companies into bankruptcy and only about half the insured value was actually repaid.

Two centuries after the British had learned their fiery lesson, postfire Chicago required that new buildings be made of brick and stone. The city went on to design buildings of metal. In 1885, the iron-framed Home Insurance Building was erected. It is considered the world's first skyscraper and led the way for the Sears Tower, one of the world's tallest buildings. The phoenix-like restoration of Chicago turned the city into the stuff of legend, an example to Americans of can-do energy, spirit, and resolve. In Chicago, as in London, fire forced a city to grow up.

*Seventeenth-century firefighting was ad hoc and volunteer. Bucket brigades tried to put out fires by throwing pail after pail of water on them, passed hand to hand from a water source.*

# Soot, Snow, and Starvation

*How an Indonesian volcano froze the world*

## Ignorance is bliss

In April 1815 few people in the West were paying attention to Mount Tambora, a volcano on the island of Sumbawa in the Dutch East Indies. Certainly the Dutch weren't. Holland was under French occupation and Britain had seized her Asian colonial possessions. England and Germany were battling Napoleon, who was only two months away from his final defeat at Waterloo. The Americans were rebuilding Washington, D.C., burned by the British the previous year at the end of the War of 1812.

Faraway Tambora would play an important role in all these countries in the coming months. It erupted, causing winterlike conditions in the Northern Hemisphere and the greatest food-production crisis in modern history.

Small, parched, and remote, Sumbawa was a minor possession in Holland's tropical empire (today's Indonesia). Two sultans ruled the land, and the inhabitants were strict Muslims. Sumbawa was best known for its two main exports: strong horses and sappan, a wood used for boatbuilding and the production of a valuable red dye. Mount Tambora was located on the north shore of the island. It had been quiet for centuries. Before the eruption it may have been as much as 13,000 feet tall.

## The big bang

On the evening of April 5, 1815, Tambora began erupting with a series of explosive shocks. Some 450 miles away in central Java, they sounded like cannon fire. On April 11 the explosions began again, shaking homes on the neighboring island of Sulawesi and filling the air there with a dense cloud of fine ash that blotted out sunlight. The major eruptions continued through April. They did not cease entirely until July.

On Sumbawa the explosions killed nearly everyone. Out of a population of 12,000, only 26 people survived. People and animals were thrown into the air. Trees were torn out of the ground. Houses were crushed by the weight of the volcanic ash. Lava gushed and a high-speed avalanche of hot, glowing ash, rock fragments, and gas—a pyroclastic flow—rushed from the crater down the mountain to the sea, incinerating anything in its path. The entire island was buried under a thick, heavy coat of ash to a depth of several feet. Two of Sumbawa's six regions were obliterated. Tambora's height was reduced by one-third.

## End of a world

Estimates of just how much ejecta Tambora discharged vary, but a good guess is 25 cubic miles. This outclasses any other eruption in recorded history. (By comparison, mighty Mount Saint Helens in Washington state poofed out a piddling 0.06 cubic miles when it erupted in 1980.) At sea the ash formed

*Mount Tambora was the largest eruption in recorded history. It blasted a huge column of ejecta high into the stratosphere, which encircled and cooled the planet. About 82,000 people died from the blast. Others around the globe starved, froze, or fell ill from the disruption of the seasons.*

immense rafts that were encountered by ships years after the eruption. On land it buried crops in depths from inches (on Java) to feet (on neighboring Lombok), depending on their distance from the volcano. This massive ash fall made agriculture nearly impossible for months throughout much of the Dutch East Indies. Without food, people starved. Weakened by famine and choked by airborne volcanic dust, they became more susceptible to all sorts of illnesses. An estimated 82,000 people in the area died in the aftermath of the explosion.

## Hawaiian for *"ouch ouch"*?

Scientists believe that volcanoes like Tambora are formed by the action of plate tectonics. This theory explains geologic processes as the movement of giant 30-mile-thick slabs of rock—tectonic plates—that form the earth's crust. These plates float on a sea of hot pressurized magma (liquid rock) that makes up the earth's mantle. The grinding of the tectonic plates over, under, and beside one another causes the movement of continents, the uplifting of mountains, the shaking of earthquakes, and the formation of volcanoes.

Volcanoes form on the edges of continents, within island chains, or along submarine mountain ranges. Tambora is part of the Pacific Ring of Fire, a string of volcanic vents at the edge of the Pacific tectonic plate.

Volcanoes are formed in these regions when magma from the mantle forces its way to the surface through cracks in the crust. Magma can either ooze or explode. As flowing lava it can reach speeds of 10 to 30 miles per hour. Depending on how fast it travels and cools, lava solidifies into two main forms, which are referred to by their Hawaiian names. Sharp-edged *aa* (for the barefooted, an appropriate term) has a rough, jagged, spiny surface, like a demolition zone.

*Pahoehoe* is lava that has solidified into a smooth, billowy, or ropy surface.

Tambora is a stratovolcano (also known as a composite volcano), one of the two main types. Such volcanoes are typically large, steep-sided symmetrical cones. They are built of alternating layers of lava, volcanic ash, cinders, and rock fragments. These are some of the most beautiful mountains on earth: Mount Fuji in Japan, Mount Cotopaxi in Ecuador, and Mount Rainier in the United States are all stratovolcanoes. Historically, stratovolcanoes are the source of the most violent eruptions; pressure builds up over decades or centuries behind a lava plug, then explodes.

Shield volcanoes, the other major type, do not explode but spew oozing streams of lava. These volcanoes, like Mauna Loa in the Hawaiian Islands, have moderate slopes formed from repeated lava flows. Internal pressure can slowly push shield volcanoes apart. Eventually they can split open. Past Hawaiian volcanic action has tumbled gigantic slabs of these unstable islands (one as big as New York City!) into the sea, sending 300-foot tsunamis racing to shores as far away as China.

## "Eighteen Hundred and Froze to Death"

Beyond Indonesia, the consequences of Tambora were also dire. Tambora's ash cloud was blown around the globe. It reflected some 30 percent of the sun's rays back into space, creating grand sunsets and lowering world temperatures in 1816 by several degrees.

Europe and North America seem to have fared the worst from this change. Crops failed, lakes remained frozen the entire year, and snow fell in July. It was

*In much of the Northern Hemisphere, crops failed, lakes remained frozen, and snow fell in July.*

"The Year Without a Summer," one of many volcanic coolings so named, but the most dramatic on record. On the North American continent, aboriginal peoples dependent on hunting and gathering starved. The Yukon in northern Canada recorded one year of continuous winter. Lakes froze to the bottom and newborn moose stuck to the ground, unable to move; when found, they were eaten on the spot. In Maine, where temperatures began to drop in June, the year 1816 was later called "Eighteen Hundred and Froze to Death" (though in fact only one documented human freezing occurred). Crops were wrecked by repeated snowfalls throughout the summer. Cattle died from lack of hay, newly shorn sheep died from cold, and people were reduced to eating wild plants and porcupines. Fifteen thousand farmers immigrated to other states, turning many Maine villages into ghost towns. Thousands left other New England states as well. This population shift, however, was a boon for the Midwest. By settling land west of the Ohio River, the migrants helped Indiana become a state in 1816 and Illinois in 1818.

Conditions were nearly as bad as far south as New York and Pennsylvania, where crops failed and songbirds fell frozen from trees. Down in Virginia, former president Thomas Jefferson was so affected by the poor corn harvest that he had to borrow a thousand dollars to keep his farm, Monticello, solvent during the barren year. Food prices rose steeply. Although some state governments intervened, the federal government did little to alleviate the problem.

## A season for monsters

Europeans also suffered. In Ireland it rained 142 out of 153 days between May and September, ruining crops. In France, as supplies dwindled and prices rose, food riots erupted. In Switzerland, where lakes remained frozen and the harvest was destroyed, provinces refused to export crops to one another. Mary Shelley, on holiday there in early June but kept indoors by the tempestuous weather and unseasonable gloom, was motivated to write her novel *Frankenstein*. Her friend Lord Byron wrote the poem "Darkness." The atmospheric murk and spectacular sunsets of 1816 may have also been the inspiration for the misty style affected by the British painter J.M.W. Turner.

The year 1816 also brought illness. An epidemic of typhus swept Europe in 1816. More than 50,000 people died in Ireland alone. Cholera first spread beyond India that year after a famine in Bengal, finally reaching Europe and America in the 1830s. Hundreds of thousands died. Cholera is spread by

*In France, as food supplies dwindled and prices rose, riots erupted and shops and warehouses were looted.*

infected water. Typhus is spread by human body lice. On a crowded, unsanitary continent whose cities were filling with hungry refugees from the country, such diseases spread easily.

At the time, many causes were suggested for the bad weather: God. Fate. Sunspots. In Milan one scholar blamed the cold on Benjamin Franklin's new invention, the lightning rod, recently installed on buildings throughout the city. Ironically, Franklin himself had suggested the volcanic connection after an eruption on Iceland in 1783 was followed by abnormally cool weather. Tambora, however, was more remote, and it was years before anyone connected the Year Without a Summer with the Sumbawan catastrophe. In 1816 news traveled slower than volcanic ash.

# King Blizzard
### How the Great White Hurricane built the subway

A.D. 1888

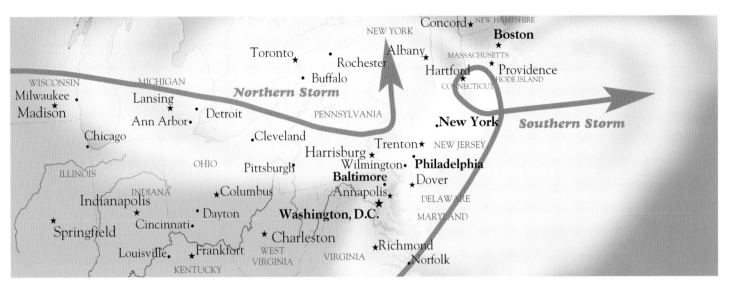

## The mother of all storms

For three long days in 1888 a snowstorm paralyzed the East Coast of the United States. The newspapers of the day competed with one another for names powerful enough to describe it. They called it the Great White Hurricane, King Blizzard, the Snow Terror. We know it today as the blizzard of 1888—and cities haven't been the same since. It altered the way we watch the weather. It changed the way we deal with emergencies. It transformed the very nature of city transportation.

## Buggy jam

The United States of 1888 was a rising industrial power. New York City was its most important metropolis, the financial and cultural center of the nation and the wonder of the industrial world. Although awe-inspiring then, it was a less imposing city than it is today. Its first skyscraper, the 26-story World Building, would not open until 1890. It was also much smaller, including just Manhattan Island. Brooklyn, the Bronx, Queens, and Staten Island (with Manhattan, today's five boroughs) would not be annexed until 1898.

But New York still had more energy, more jobs, and more money than any place else. The nation's wealthiest families provided the cash. They enjoyed lives of breathtaking splendor in palatial homes that lined the city's fanciest streets. The country's growing pool of impoverished immigrants provided the labor. The lucky ones were crowded into poorly built, unheated, vermin-infested tenements. The unlucky lived on the streets. Thousands of newcomers poured in every day, hungry for work.

Transportation into this mecca was a complicated ballet, with hundreds of train departures and arrivals every day at Grand Central Depot, traffic flowing in across the newly completed Brooklyn Bridge, and ferries running at five-minute intervals on the Hudson and East rivers. This network got workers, goods, and food in and out.

Transit within the city was a mess. Except for the steam- and electric-powered elevated trains, all transport was on surface streets. It was a snarl of plodding horse-drawn carts and crawling street railroads.

## What's that smell?

Walking was faster—if you dared. Streets were mounded with horse manure (half a million pounds had to be disposed of every day) and awash in rivers of horse urine (60,000 gallons a day). Although the New York City Department of Street Cleaning had been created in 1881 in response to the public up-roar over street litter and disorganized garbage collection, there were as yet no anti-litter laws. Trash was everywhere.

Disease was rampant, too, despite a city Board of Health that had been around since 1803. Tuberculosis, pneumonia, and intestinal diarrhea were the major killers. Poor sanitation ensured that repeated epidemics of cholera killed thousands.

*From Virginia to Canada, communication ceased. Boston, Philadelphia, New York, and Washington, D.C., were completely shut down, cut off from the rest of the country.*

*The storm froze the East River, stopping ferry traffic. Briefly, the solid surface allowed some people to walk from Manhattan to the opposite bank, before the ice broke up and swept the less nimble out to sea.*

## Scofflaw central

New York's communication system was also a lawless anarchy. A crisscrossing spiderweb of telegraph lines, phone wires, and electrical cables canopied the streets. An 1886 law mandated the burial of all aboveground wires, but it was simply ignored by the private companies that owned and maintained the lines. Wooden line poles were 50 to 150 feet high, some with as many as 200 wires.

Such problems were not unique to New York. Other American cities suffered similar difficulties. But as the most dynamic and crowded of all American metropolises, Manhattan's problems were especially glaring.

Alfred Ely Beach, editor of *Scientific American* magazine, had proposed a solution to the traffic problem. Since 1849 he had been crusading for an underground railroad as an alternative to surface traffic jams. He even built a hugely popular test tunnel in 1870. But for years Tammany Hall had crushed all subway legislation. Tammany was the political ring that controlled city government. It stole from the city treasury, bribed city newspapers for reverential coverage, and took rake-offs from surface transportation. The trash, disease, and wiring problems were also largely its fault.

## Forecast: sunny and fair...

On the evening of Saturday, March 10, 1888, two massive storm systems were moving toward this complex, fragile, ill-governed city. One, laden with superchilled air from Canada, was dumping snow across the Midwest. The other was heading up the Atlantic from the south, loaded with moisture. The United States Army Signal Corps, the federal body responsible for weather forecasting, was aware of both storms. The corps monitored weather conditions at stations across the country. Temperature readings, barometric pressure, wind speed, and direction were all telegraphed to Washington, D.C., where the data was analyzed and forecasts were issued. The corps believed that neither storm posed any danger to the eastern seaboard. When the Saturday evening forecast was issued, it predicted a continuation of the pleasant springlike weather of the previous week: fair, brisk, perhaps a little rain. On Sunday, the Signal Corps took the day off.

## Correction: gigantic blizzard

By Sunday afternoon, the two storms had collided over Long Island. Drawing on each other's power, they became a gigantic blizzard. Any snowstorm with winds of at least 35 miles per hour and temperatures of 20 degrees Fahrenheit or lower can be termed a blizzard. This storm dropped the temperature to below zero. Winds were clocked at 75 to 85 miles per hour. Snowfall was extraordinary. Electric and telegraph lines broke. Street trash and signs ripped from walls turned into deadly projectiles. Transportation stopped: trains, carriages, ships, and ferries were all literally snowed under. Boston, Philadelphia, New York, and Washington, D.C., were completely shut down, cut off from the rest of the country. President Grover Cleveland was stranded in his country home outside the capital, unable to contact his cabinet or Congress. From Virginia to Canada, contact with the outside world ceased.

On March 14 the storms finally moved on. One headed north to Greenland, the other into the Atlantic. (It eventually reached Europe, where it was known as "the American Storm.") Houses and trains were buried under drifts 50 feet deep. At least 400 people died, frozen in drifts, killed by windblown debris, drowned in rivers and lakes, or electrocuted by fallen wires. Untold hundreds were lost at sea. Jetties and piers up and down the coast were damaged by waves that had reached 50 to 70 feet high. Two hundred ships sank.

## Throw the bums out!

By paralyzing—and embarrassing—the young nation's most influential cities, the storm revealed the frailty of industrial life and the dependence of cities on roads, trains, and telegraph lines. The storm roused public dissatisfaction and sparked waves of reform, particularly in New York City.

Before the storm of 1888, city emergency relief was ad hoc; snow removal was an individual responsibility. After the storm, New York's snowbound streets were clotted with snapped wire poles and sizzling high-voltage lines. With enraged public opinion behind him, reform mayor Abram Hewitt forced the communication and power companies to begin burying lines. To get traffic moving, 17,000 temporary workers removed snow from main thoroughfares and railway cuts. Hewitt also pushed through the long-delayed subway legislation. Despite these moves, New Yorkers were unhappy with the city government's slowness in responding. For too long, businesses were unable to get supplies in or products out. Nor were upstate farmers able to get their milk or butter to market. Hewitt, already unpopular, was voted out in November.

Other politicians took note. By 1894 all New York wires were underground. By 1904 the Interborough Rapid Transit Company opened the first 22 miles of the New York subway. The speedy, all-weather, and traffic-proof form of transportation was immediately popular among all classes of New Yorkers. About 150,000 people rode the very first day. Other companies started their own lines. Today the combined system covers 722 miles.

## Storm of reform

Many other East Coast cities followed suit, burying wires, building underground railroads, and instituting other reforms. Today nearly all American cities take some responsibility for litter cleanup, snow removal, and emergency planning. The city emergency plans that clicked into place after the September 11, 2001, terrorist attack on New York's World Trade Center had their origins in the blizzard of 1888.

The Army was not forgiven for its uncommonly poor weather forecast. In 1891 the Signal Corps was transferred to the Department of Agriculture. The name was changed to the United States Weather Bureau. The reformed agency—now on watch 24/7—was charged not just with daily weather prediction, but long-range forecasting. It was the beginning of serious American efforts to understand how weather works.

*King Blizzard showed New Yorkers the need for weatherproof transportation. The New York subway, opened in 1904, was an immediate success; 150,000 people rode the first day.*

# When the Catfish Shakes

## How the Great Kanto Quake rebuilt the world

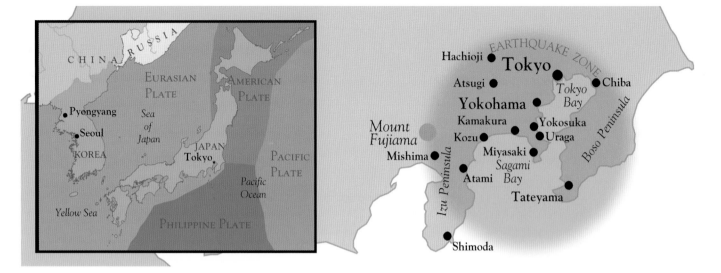

## Sayonara to all that

In 1923 a monstrous earthquake struck the Kanto plain of Japan. It left two cities in ruins: Tokyo, the capital, and Yokohama, the most important port. The damage and aftermath contributed to the economic collapse of Asia's most prosperous and modern country and plunged Japan into a quest for empire that led to war and, ultimately, calamitous defeat. The effects of the quake are still with us today in architecture, engineering, and emergency preparedness.

## Good for business

World War I was bad for Europe but good for Japan. Between 1914 and 1918, that European conflict killed 34 million people, destroyed the Austro-Hungarian and Ottoman empires, wrecked the German economy, and laid the foundations for both World War II and today's Balkan and Palestinian strife. Japan, however, used the European war as an opportunity to enhance its position as Asia's preeminent power. Japan had already astounded the world by defeating Russia in 1903. The country had annexed Korea in 1912. Now it occupied Manchuria and seized Germany's Asian colonies in China and the Pacific.

Meanwhile, Japanese export industries moved into India and Southeast Asia, markets that preoccupied Europe was ignoring. Japan also supplied the warring Europeans with products they could no longer make themselves. By the end of the war Japan was a major exporter of ships, textiles, and munitions. Japan had a substantial merchant fleet and an impressive military machine. Most importantly, it had international prestige nearly on a par with France, Britain, and the United States. By 1923 exports were booming, incomes were rising, and the middle class was growing.

## Up to code

In 1853 American commodore Matthew Perry had forced Japan to open to foreign trade. By 1923 the country was only 70 years into the process of transforming from a feudal kingdom to a modern state. But Tokyo and Yokohama were state-of-the-art cities. They boasted efficient rail systems, electric lighting, and multistory office buildings made of concrete, stone, and steel. Foreign architects such as Frank Lloyd Wright and Bruno Taut had designed landmark buildings there.

Both cities, however, also had large traditional Japanese neighborhoods with one- and two-story wooden houses, roofed with tiles. Post-and-beam frames supported these buildings. Walls were made of wood and sliding wood-and-paper shoji screens.

*During the quake the ground rippled like ocean waves. In Motomachi, the Japanese section of Yokohama, wooden frames of traditional buildings jackknifed inward or were pancaked flat by their tile roofs. The Hundred Steps leading up to a foreign settlement collapsed with the hillside.*

## Death in the afternoon

All these buildings were put to the severest of tests by the Great Kanto Earthquake.

On Saturday, September 1, 1923, at 11:23 A.M., the first quake struck. It lasted four minutes. The ground heaved and roiled like ocean waves. Streets split. Hillsides collapsed. Water mains broke. Telegraph and telephone lines snapped. Chemical and fuel storage tanks burst. Wooden houses splintered, jackknifed, and pancaked. Stone and brick structures were ground to rubble. Some 200 aftershocks followed the initial quake, including another major event at 11:47 A.M. on Sunday, followed by 300 more aftershocks. The vibrations also generated a 39-foot tsunami and multiple landslides.

No sooner had the initial shaking subsided than Japan learned the same deadly lesson as London and Chicago before it. Lunchtime fire braziers, overturned by the quake, set ruins alight in both Tokyo and Yokohama. Eighty-eight fires started simultaneously in Yokohama alone. Aided by hot weather, fed by spilled fuel, driven by strong winds, the flames quickly spread into an unstoppable conflagration. Wooden homes that had survived the initial destruction became blazing coffins. Survivors who had huddled with their remaining possessions in open areas were set alight and suffocated by the engulfing flames.

In all, 3.4 million people were affected by the quake, in which 140,000 people died and 694,000 homes were destroyed. Property damage exceeded one billion dollars.

*Immediately after the quake, overturned charcoal braziers set ruins alight, turning wooden homes that had come through the initial shaking intact into blazing coffins.*

## Shaky plates

Most earthquakes are believed to be caused by the movement of tectonic plates, the grinding, halting motion of the dynamic jigsaw puzzle that makes up the earth's crust. The motion creates powerful shock waves that shake everything they pass through: earth, water, trees, buildings, and people. Although plate tectonics does not account for all earthquakes (some occur far from plate boundaries), the theory works well for Japan, which is at the edge of three plate boundaries. The explanation is certainly more plausible than the traditional Japanese story, which blames the shaking on the antics of a giant catfish! Each year Japan suffers an average of 1,000 earthquakes of varying intensities, plus periodic volcanic eruptions (another tectonic side effect). The Kanto Quake was centered in Sagami Bay. Afterward, a survey of the sea floor reported several new ridges 180 to 300 feet high along a submarine volcanic chain. On land several areas rose as much as 24 feet, then subsided.

Earthquakes can be measured by seismographs. The first such device was developed in A.D. 132 by Chang Heng, a Chinese court official. John Milne, a British scientist who studied earthquakes in Japan during the 1880s, invented the precursor to modern seismographs. Both the Chinese and British devices use a pendulum that moves when shaken.

Several methods have been developed to measure

and compare the size of earthquakes. Most commonly used is the Richter scale, invented by Charles Richter in 1935. The Richter scale calculates the magnitude of an earthquake from the vibrations recorded on a seismograph. An increase of one on the scale corresponds to a tenfold increase in the size of a quake. Thus, a magnitude 8 quake is 10 times more powerful than a magnitude 7 and 100 times more powerful than a magnitude 6. The Great Kanto Earthquake was a magnitude 7.9. By comparison, the Gujarat, India, earthquake of 2001 was a magnitude 8.3. The San Francisco earthquake of 1906 was a magnitude 8.25.

## It's *their* fault

The economic and social consequences of the Great Kanto Earthquake were devastating. In the days immediately after the quake, false rumors that local Koreans were poisoning wells and planning a takeover resulted in anti-Korean riots and murders. Martial law was declared. With factories and businesses destroyed, unemployment in the Kanto region rose to nearly 50 percent. Although substantial emergency foreign aid arrived immediately after the quake, foreign investment to help rebuild the economy was timid. Banks failed. Recovery was painfully slow.

These problems helped precipitate the Showa financial crisis, a 1927 economic slump that preceded the worldwide Great Depression of the 1930s. Many Japanese lost faith in Western-style economics and political organization. They turned inward, to older traditions, and looked to their successful military for leadership. By 1940 Japan's democratic government was replaced by a hysterically antiforeign, anticolonial, one-party state. The new leadership, dedicated to the worship of the emperor and military power, pursued an aggressive expansionist strategy designed to capture supplies of cheap labor and raw materials throughout Asia. The policy put the country on a collision course with Asia's established (and no less exploitative) colonial powers: England, Holland, France, and the United States. The opposing sides went to war—World War II—with Japan the early winner but the ultimate loser.

## Ready for the big one

The Great Kanto Earthquake ushered in the age of modern earthquake engineering. The World Engineering Congress of 1929 was held in Tokyo, with earthquake-resistant construction the main topic of discussion. Japanese building codes were revised so that reinforced concrete and steel buildings could better withstand another powerful quake. The height of wooden and brick buildings was limited. Tile-roof designs were made safer. These ideas became the basis for new earthquake-resistant building designs used in cities around the world. When a modern building survives an earthquake intact, it owes something to the harsh lessons taught by the Great Kanto Earthquake.

Since 1923, Japan has become one of the most earthquake-aware countries in the world. Japanese schoolchildren practice earthquake evacuation drills every September 1, the anniversary of the Great Kanto Earthquake. Some Japanese still remember the event and the date of the Great Kanto Earthquake with this device: *Jishin hito-yure kuni sanzan* ("earthquake one big shake, country is in ruins"). *Hito* means one. *Ku* (from *kuni*) means nine. *Ni* means two. *San* (from *sanzan*) means three. Thus, 1-9-2-3.

*Steel-reinforced concrete buildings endured both the shaking and the fire best of all. This structure, the Kokugikan (the National Sumo Wrestling Center) in Ryogoku district, not only survived the quake but stood until 1983.*

# Boiling the Frog
*How business as usual invites future disasters*

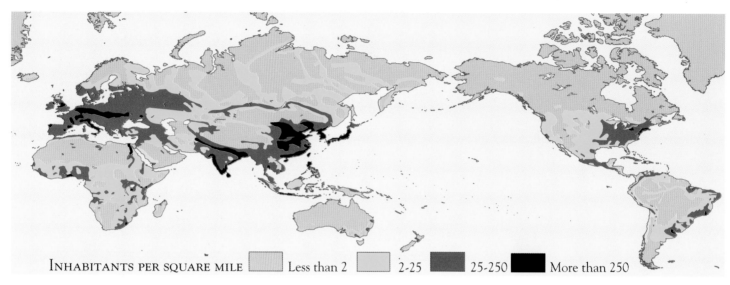

INHABITANTS PER SQUARE MILE — Less than 2 — 2-25 — 25-250 — More than 250

## No place to hide

We live on a dangerous planet.

If the past is any guide, our future will be punctuated by more natural disasters, from earthquakes to floods to comet and meteor impacts. Some will surely have as great an effect on human history as those described in this book.

In all probability the disasters of the future will be worse than those of the past. This is our doing. One billion people lived on the earth in 1800. World population grew to two billion in 1930, three billion in 1960, and four billion in 1975. Over six billion people are here now; five more are born every second. If present trends of rising population continue, 10 to 15 billion people will be squeezed onto the earth's surface by the next century. Demographers project that the population may then stabilize.

Human beings now occupy 83 percent of the earth's land area to live on, farm, mine, or fish. By filling so much space on our planet's surface, we may increase the impact of natural disasters. Hardly any place on earth is left where a tsunami, a volcanic eruption, or a blizzard can strike without hurting someone. Simply put, more of us are here to get in the way.

Look at China. Densely populated for thousands of years, it is also cursed with repeated earthquakes and floods that have killed tens of millions of people. More and more of the world is reaching China-style population densities. Giant earthquakes hit the Mississippi River Valley in 1811 and 1812, when the region was sparsely settled. Millions live there now. The probability of another major quake hitting the area by 2040 is 90 percent.

## How fast can *you* run?

Millions also live near Mount Rainier, America's most dangerous volcano. Rainier has repeatedly spewed out enormous *lahars* (volcanic mudflows), several within historical times. The worst was the massive Osceola mudflow 5,600 years ago. It inundated over 100 square miles of Puget Sound, filling valleys now covered with towns to a depth of 300 feet and reaching what is now Seattle. Unlike Japan, which has invested heavily in debris walls and other landslide-diversion systems, towns on the slopes of Mount Rainier are depending on early warning and evacuation. They plan to wait for the rumbles, then run.

Millions more people live on the East Coast of North America. Across the Atlantic is Cumbre Vieja, a geologically unstable volcano in the Canary Islands. If an eruption triggers one of its deeply fissured flanks to slide into the sea, the resulting mega-tsunami would drown the eastern seaboard of North America as far as 12 miles inland. Forty million people would be inundated.

## Tilting the balance

But there's worse. While our increased presence makes the impact of natural disasters larger, our industrial civilization actually adds to their power and recurrence. The way we live is affecting temperature, climate, weather, and perhaps even the frequency and magnitude of earthquakes.

The life of an industrial citizen creates an enormous

*Global warming may bring higher sea levels that will flood many low-lying coastal cities.*

wake of global cause and effect—resources used and pollution spread. Collectively we are changing the earth in unintended ways.

The atmosphere is getting hotter. Most atmospheric scientists agree that the tons of extra carbon dioxide and other greenhouse gases pumped into the air by our cars and factories are part of the problem. At the very least, they are a contributing factor to a cyclic change. At worst, they are the primary cause.

We also know our climate is becoming less stable, our weather more extreme. Rainfall patterns are changing. Droughts and floods are becoming more intense. Hurricanes and other storms are becoming more destructive. Climatic conditions we've thought of as normal are beginning to change.

Today the American Midwest supports vast farms of wheat, corn, and soybeans. A century from now the deserts of northern Mexico may have moved into Kansas, while the continent's breadbasket may relocate to Saskatchewan, in Canada. The political consequences of such a change would be impressive.

Some scientists have suggested that pollution from factories and power stations in North America and Europe might counter global warming. These emissions fill the air with aerosol particles that tend to scatter sunlight and form clouds, cooling the Northern Hemisphere. But because there has to be a rough balance between the heat in the Northern and Southern Hemispheres, this cooling pushes the point of "thermal equilibrium" south. With it go the rain clouds that people depend on to grow crops in Africa's drought-prone Sahel. Over the past 30 years this has contributed to one of the longest droughts in history, massive crop failures, and over a million deaths due to starvation. In the future, as China industrializes, the same aerosol effect could weaken the monsoon, impacting harvests in India.

More intense droughts will create bigger forest fires.

Recall that the fires of London, Chicago, and Tokyo all occurred during hot, dry summers. Though they are considered historic because of their effect on human lives and property, these city fires pale to insignificance when compared with some of our planet's truly big forest fires in China, the United States, Indonesia, and Australia. They eat up millions of acres and impair the health of entire continents.

## Nevada beachfront?

Probably the most discussed effect of global warming is the expected rise in sea level. This will come from the melting of polar ice and glacial ice sheets, plus the swelling of the oceans due to heating. Already Arctic Ocean ice is just half as thick as it was in 1958 and covers less area. The Antarctic is also shrinking, losing chunks the size of Rhode Island. Plants are now growing in parts of the Antarctic that have been frozen in the past.

Currently, sea level is rising one inch or so every decade. A catastrophic loss of polar ice could raise sea levels by 30 feet or more. Higher sea levels will inundate many low-lying coastal cities such as New Orleans and Bangkok. Southern Florida and island countries such as the Maldives will disappear. Farmland will be transformed into saltwater marsh, and the aquifers we depend on for irrigation and drinking water will turn brackish.

Because of our love of large dams (to store water for drinking, for irrigation, and for industry as well as for hydroelectric power), we may get more frequent earthquakes. Dams impound huge volumes of water. In seismically active areas, the weight of the water and seepage into tectonic faults may cause the earth to move, a phenomenon known as reservoir-induced seismicity. In extreme cases it may cause the dam to fail, adding catastrophic flooding to earthquake damage. India's gigantic Sardar Sarovar Dam is in an

earthquake zone. So is China's Three Gorges Dam, which, when completed, will be the world's largest. Their impounded waters will also displace millions of people and animals.

## So long, farewell, *auf Wiedersehen,* good-bye

Our inescapable presence everywhere on the globe has caused a drastic reduction in other species. Some scientists call this the fifth great extinction. Extinction is part of natural selection, of course. Ninety percent of the species that have ever existed are now gone. But the rate of animal and plant extinction since our population started growing seems to be rising.

Some biologists guess that as many as 100 plant and animal species could be vanishing per day. By the end of the twenty-first century, virtually all inhabitable land will be either city or farmland. By the time the human population tops out, half the species of plants and animals present now may be gone. All large wild mammals outside of zoos and game preserves may disappear, forever. Those creatures that survive will be the "weedy" species that thrive on disturbed habitat: crows, starlings, rats, coyotes, cockroaches. It will be a poorer world: a human monoculture.

Our situation is like the famous parable of the boiling frog. If dropped in a pot of boiling water, it will leap to safety. If placed in a container of cold water that is gradually heated to boiling, it will stoically cook to death. We are wreaking havoc on our home, but too slowly to be startled into action.

### There's hope

This impoverished, disaster-prone future is not inevitable. We can change the way we live. Most importantly, we can reduce our population by having fewer children. That would allow more of us to live outside our planet's most disaster-prone areas, allow us to use the land less intensely, and save some wild spaces for our nonhuman neighbors.

We can learn to do with less, particularly less of the fossil fuels that hasten the greenhouse effect. We can redesign our cities to reduce sprawl and encourage public transportation, biking, and walking. We can start powering cities with clean, renewable resources like solar, wind, and tidal energy. We can plant gardens and forests on our roofs.

Individually, we can replace our reliance on the internal combustion engine and drive more efficient, less polluting cars like hybrid gas-electrics. Better, we can drive zero-emission hydrogen-fuel-cell vehicles, whose only waste product is water vapor. Better yet, we can walk or ride bicycles. We can switch from electricity-hogging incandescent bulbs—little changed since the age of Edison—to efficient compact fluorescents, which use a quarter of an incandescent's power for the same light and last for nearly a decade. Even better, we can move up to the more miserly light-emitting diodes. Little banks of these tiny lights produce as much illumination as a conventional bulb on minuscule amounts of power; such technology has been used for years in solar-powered homes.

In everything we buy we can insist on less packaging and less advertising, thus cutting our need for energy, for raw materials, and for landfills. We can buy locally made products, reducing the need for distant sweatshop labor. We can boycott fast food, which produces mountains of garbage and destroys vital rainforest land to produce beef cattle. We can compost. We can recycle.

Some politicians and corporate leaders already dismiss such goals. Their wealth and power depend on things staying as they are. They depend on our passivity. They depend on business as usual.

But make no mistake, even small changes in the way we lead our lives can help slow the environmental processes that are making disasters worse and our home less hospitable. They may be difficult. They may cost us money. They may seem uncool to the uninformed. But they could help ensure our survival.

That would really change history.

*As many as 100 plant and animal species may be vanishing per day.*

# BIBLIOGRAPHY

*For Younger Readers*

Bortz, Fred
  *Collision Course: Cosmic Impacts and Life on Earth*
  Brookfield, Connecticut: Millbrook Press
  2001

Kahl, Jonathan D.
  *National Audubon Society First Field Guide: Weather*
  New York: Scholastic Inc.
  1998

Murphy, Jim
  *Blizzard!*
  New York: Scholastic Inc.
  2000

Silverstein, Alvin; Silverstein, Virginia; Silverstein, Laura Nunn
  *Plate Tectonics*
  Brookfield, Connecticut: Millbrook Press
  1998

Vogel, Carole G.
  *Nature's Fury*
  New York: Scholastic Inc.
  2000

*For Older Readers*

Alvarez, Walter
  *T. Rex and the Crater of Doom*
  Princeton, New Jersey: Princeton University Press
  1997

Coontz, Robert, et al.
  "Nine Days That Shook the World"
  *New Scientist*
  August 7, 1999

Dennis, Jerry
  *It's Raining Frogs and Fishes*
  New York: HarperCollins
  1992

Packe, Michael; Seaman, L.C.B., ed.
  *King Edward III*
  London: Routledge Kegan and Paul
  1983

Pellegrino, Charles
  *Unearthing Atlantis: An Archaeological Odyssey to the Fabled
    Lost Civilization*
  New York: Avon Books
  2001

Phillipson, David W.
  *Ancient Ethiopia: Aksum, Its Antecedents and Successors*
  London: British Museum Press
  1998

Poole, Otis Manchester
  *The Death of Old Yokohama in the Great Japanese Earthquake of
    September 1, 1923*
  London: George Allen and Unwin Ltd.
  1968

Reader, John
  *Africa: A Biography of the Continent*
  New York: Alfred A. Knopf
  1997

Robinson, Andrew
  *Earth Shock: Hurricanes, Volcanoes, Earthquakes, Tornadoes,
    and Other Forces of Nature*
  London and New York: Thames & Hudson
  1993

Stommel, Elizabeth; Stommel, Henry
  *Volcano Weather: The Story of 1816, the Year Without a
    Summer*
  Newport, Rhode Island: Seven Seas Press
  1995

Turnbull, Stephen
  *The Samurai Sourcebook*
  London: Cassell and Company
  1998

Winters, Harold A., et al.
  *Battling the Elements: Weather and Terrain in the Conduct of
    War*
  Baltimore: Johns Hopkins University Press
  2001

*Web Sites*

Cameron, Carol; James, Charles
  *The 1923 Great Kanto Earthquake and Fire*
  http://nisee.berkeley.edu/kanto/yokohama.html
  National Information Service for Earthquake Engineering
  University of California, Berkeley

Caraway, William M.
  *Korea: In the Eye of the Tiger*
  http://www.koreanhistoryproject.org
  Korean History Project
  2001

Pirman, David
  *The New York Subway: Its Construction and Equipment*
  http://www.nycsubway.org/irt/irtbook/
  Interborough Rapid Transit
  1995

Robinson, Bruce
  *Red Sky at Night: Before and After the Great Fire*
  http://www.bbc.co.uk/history/society_culture/society/great_
    fire_01.shtml
  British Broadcasting Service
  2001

Smith, Carl
  *The Great Chicago Fire and the Web of Memory*
  http://www.chicagohs.org/fire/
  Chicago Historical Society
  Northwestern University, Chicago
  1996

Toshiya Ichinose
  *Earthquake—One Big Shake and the Country Was in Ruins: The
    Great Kanto Earthquake of 1923*
  http://www.rekihaku.ac.jp/e-rekihaku/109/
  Historical Research Department, National Museum of
    Japanese History
  2001

# GLOSSARY

*aa*   Hawaiian word for rough, sharp-edged lava rock

**avian dinosaurs**   birds

*cenote*   (pronounced *say-NO-tay*, derived from the Mayan word *dzonot*, which means "sacred well") A depression or cave found in the limestone rock of Mexico's Yucatán Peninsula. Created by naturally acidic groundwater seeping through cracks in the harder surface rock that dissolves softer rock beneath.

**Cenozoic Era**   one of several great time divisions of the earth's history lasting from 65 million years ago to the present. It has two subdivisions, the *Tertiary Period*, lasting from 65 million years ago to 1.8 million years ago, and the *Quaternary Period*, lasting from 1.8 million years ago to the present. The Quaternary is further subdivided into the Pleistocene, an era of ice ages that lasted from 1.8 million years ago to 11,000 years ago, and the modern era.

**composite volcano**   see *stratovolcano*

**Cretaceous Period**   The last subdivision of the *Mesozoic Era*, lasting from 146 to 65 million years ago. Like all subdivisions of the Mesozoic, the Cretaceous is subdivided into smaller time periods that are grouped into Early, Middle, and Late. In the rock record, the end of the Cretaceous is marked by the *K-T boundary*.

**cyclone**   enormous, high-speed rotating tropical storm. Called a typhoon in the east Pacific and a hurricane in the Atlantic and the west Pacific.

**cynodont**   a broad group of extinct mammal-like reptiles that were most numerous from 222 million to about 215 million years ago, during the *Triassic Period*. They are the direct ancestors of present-day mammals.

**dinosaur**   an extinct reptilian subgroup of the archosaurs (ruling reptiles) that lived from the Late *Triassic Period* to the end of the *Mesozoic Era*. Archosaurs also include the extinct pterosaurs (flying reptiles) and two groups that have survived into the modern era: crocodiles and birds.

**earthquake**   a trembling or undulation of the earth's crust due to the faulting of the underlying rock, movement of tectonic plates, or volcanic action

**ejecta**   material thrown out of a volcano during an eruption. Ejecta can range from fine ash and gases to strands of volcanic glass to molten lava bombs to solid rock blocks.

**firebreak**   a strip of land that has been cleared to prevent the spread of fire

**graupel**   the smallest type of *hail*

**hail**   small masses or pellets of ice or frozen vapor that fall during showers or storms

**Jurassic Period**   the middle subdivision of the *Mesozoic Era*, beginning 210 million years ago and lasting for 70 million years. During this period dinosaurs became most diverse and dominant. Named for the Jura Mountains on the Franco-Swiss border, where rocks of this age were first studied.

**K-T boundary**   a thin rock layer rich in the element iridium that marks the end of the *Cretaceous Period* and the beginning of the *Tertiary Period*. Also known as the Cretaceous-Tertiary boundary. The *K* of K-T comes from the German word for chalk.

**lahar**   volcanic mudflow, made of volcanic debris and water, caused by eruption or earthquake

**lapilli**   small volcanic *ejecta*

**magma**   hot liquefied rock that makes up the earth's mantle, the region beneath the crust

**Mesozoic Era**   one of several great time divisions of earth history. *Mesozoic* means "middle animal." The Mesozoic lasted from 245 million years ago, the *Permian* extinction, to the beginning of the *Cretaceous*, 65 million years ago, when all *non-avian dinosaurs* disappeared.

**non-avian dinosaurs**   extinct *dinosaurs*

**nucleus**   an airborne particle, usually dust, required to start a hailstone

**Oort cloud**   a region of comets and other icy objects surrounding the solar system

*pahoehoe*   Hawaiian word for smooth-surfaced, ropy lava rock

**Paleozoic Era**   one of several great time divisions of earth history, lasting from 554 million years ago, when multicelled life experienced a dramatic increase in diversity, to the Great Dying at the end of the *Permian Period*, 245 million years ago, when 90 percent of all life was wiped out

**Permian Period**   the last subdivision of the *Paleozoic Era*, lasting from 286 to 245 million years ago and ended by the greatest mass extinction in the earth's history, the Great Dying. The *Permian* extinction, possibly the result of a cosmic impact, had its greatest effect on sea life. It ended the dominance of the *trilobites*.

**plate tectonics**   theory explaining the dynamic interaction of the plates that make up the earth's crust

**pumice**   frothy volcanic *ejecta* made of large volumes of air mixed with rock

**pyroclastic**   *pyro* = fire; *clastic* = movement. A type of high-speed volcanic *ejecta* made up of hot gas, air, and rock particles.

**Quaternary Period**   see *Cenozoic Era*

**shield volcano**   a gentle-sloped volcano formed by repeated lava flows

**stratovolcano**   explosive, steep-sided volcano formed by alternating layers of lava, dust, and cinders. Also called a composite volcano.

**submarine**   *sub* = under; *marine* = water. Underwater.

**Tertiary Period**   see *Cenozoic Era*

**Triassic Period**   the first subdivision of the *Mesozoic Era*, beginning 245 million years ago, after the *Permian* extinction, and ending 208 million years ago. *Dinosaurs* first appeared in the Triassic.

**trilobites**   hard-shelled, segmented creatures that existed over 300 million years ago in the ancient seas of the *Paleozoic Era*. One of the key signature creatures of the Paleozoic, they became extinct in the Great Dying at the end of the *Permian Period*.

**tsunami**   Japanese for "harbor wave." Chain of large, high-speed waves emanating from a seismic disturbance such as an earthquake, volcanic eruption, extraterrestrial impact, or landslide.

*For William Pène du Bois, whose twenty-one balloons got me started*

**Acknowledgments**

Many people made this book possible.
Two deserve star billing. Isabel Warren-Lynch, art director at Crown Books for Young
Readers, not only created the sleek design for *Dangerous Planet* but also first suggested I try my
hand at a book about disasters. Michelle Frey edited my words with rigor, patience,
and good cheer. She kept me on topic and out of blind alleys.
I also received assistance from Min-chih Chou and Yanyan Sun of the University of
Washington; Denis Twitchett of Princeton University; Mata Mahakur of the Indian Institute
of Tropical Meteorology and Dr. U. S. De of the Indian Meteorological Department; Kenneth
Cutler of Indiana University; David Green, formerly of the University of St. Andrews;
Stephen Self of the Open University; Yolanda de Jong; Bruce Houghton;
and Haruo Murakami.
Writing and illustrating this book was made easier by the generosity of Sam Connery, who
provided essential reference material, and Paul Chadwick, who helped me hone early drafts of
the chapters and gave my paintings many an invaluable critique.
My wife, Rebecca, helped me polish my text and, with my daughter, Wynn, and my son,
Parks, supported this project from beginning to end. Their enthusiastic encouragement made
creating this book a pleasure.

Text and illustrations copyright © 2003 by Bryn Barnard

Published by Crown Publishers, an imprint of Random House Children's Books,
a division of Random House, Inc., New York.

CROWN and colophon are trademarks of Random House, Inc.
www.randomhouse.com/kids

*Library of Congress Cataloging-in-Publication Data*
Barnard, Bryn.
Dangerous planet : natural disasters that changed history / Bryn Barnard.
        p. cm.
Summary: Describes specific occurrences of natural disasters, such as meteor impacts, landslides, typhoons, volcanic eruptions, and earthquakes, and their impact on human history.
Includes bibliographical references, glossary.
ISBN 0-375-82249-6 (trade) — ISBN 0-375-92249-0 (lib. bdg.)
1. Natural disasters—Juvenile literature. [1. Natural disasters.] I. Title.

GB5019.B36 2003
363.34—dc21                                                     2002017545

MANUFACTURED IN CHINA

First Edition

August 2003

10 9 8 7 6 5 4 3 2 1